1 NEPHI, CHAPTER 15
BETWEEN 600 AND 592 B.C.
AND IT CAME TO PASS THAT AFTER I, NEPHI, HAD BEEN SHOWN MANY THINGS BY THE ANGEL OF THE LORD, I RETURNED TO THE TENT OF MY FATHER.
FATHER FAVORS NEPHI--EVEN SAM. HE CONDEMNS US FOR NO REASON. I ***HATE*** HIM!

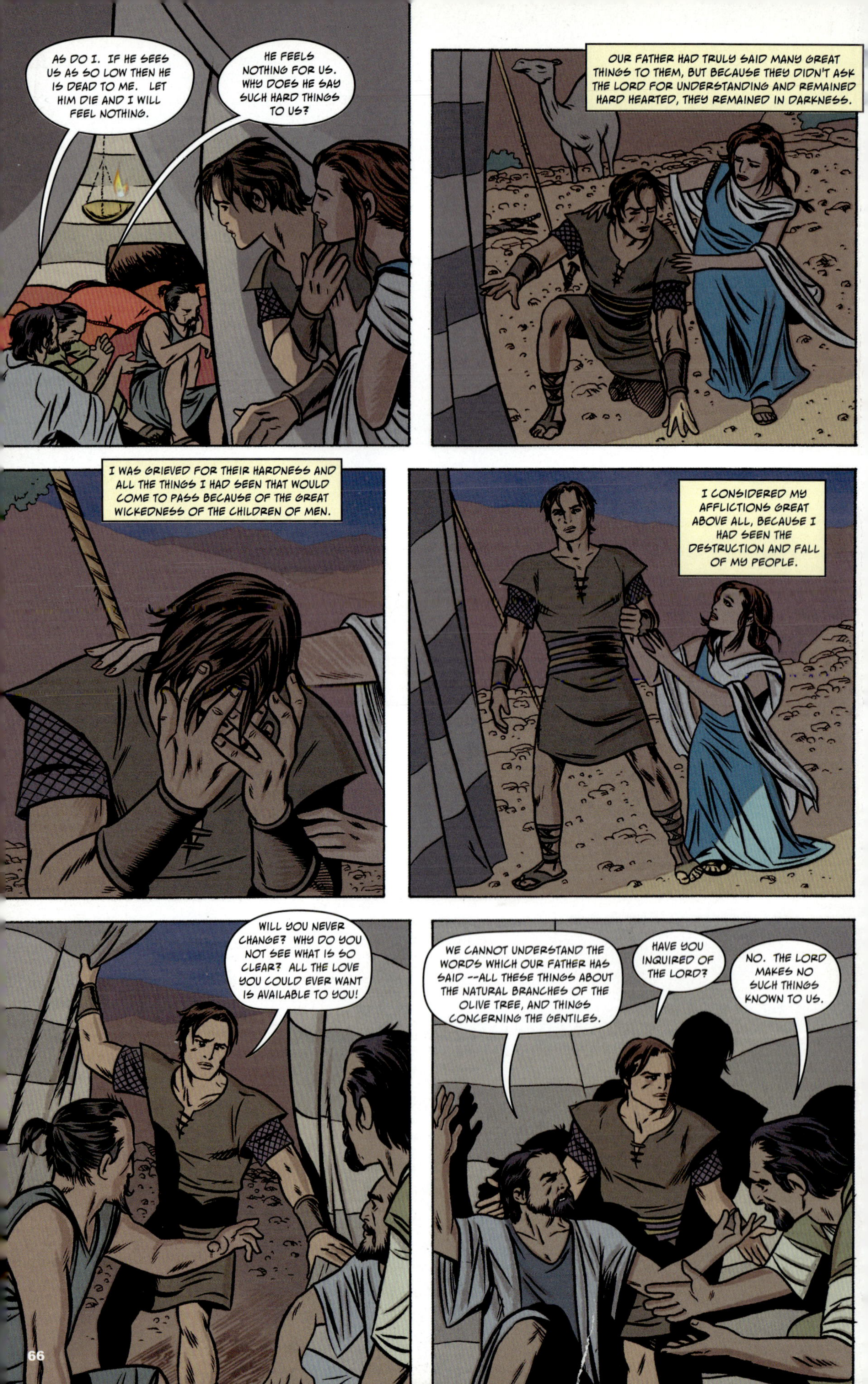
AS DO I. IF HE SEES US AS SO LOW THEN HE IS DEAD TO ME. LET HIM DIE AND I WILL FEEL NOTHING.
HE FEELS NOTHING FOR US. WHY DOES HE SAY SUCH HARD THINGS TO US?
OUR FATHER HAD TRULY SAID MANY GREAT THINGS TO THEM, BUT BECAUSE THEY DIDN'T ASK THE LORD FOR UNDERSTANDING AND REMAINED HARD HEARTED, THEY REMAINED IN DARKNESS.
I WAS GRIEVED FOR THEIR HARDNESS AND ALL THE THINGS I HAD SEEN THAT WOULD COME TO PASS BECAUSE OF THE GREAT WICKEDNESS OF THE CHILDREN OF MEN.
I CONSIDERED MY AFFLICTIONS GREAT ABOVE ALL, BECAUSE I HAD SEEN THE DESTRUCTION AND FALL OF MY PEOPLE.
WILL YOU NEVER CHANGE? WHY DO YOU NOT SEE WHAT IS SO CLEAR? ALL THE LOVE YOU COULD EVER WANT IS AVAILABLE TO YOU!
WE CANNOT UNDERSTAND THE WORDS WHICH OUR FATHER HAS SAID --ALL THESE THINGS ABOUT THE NATURAL BRANCHES OF THE OLIVE TREE, AND THINGS CONCERNING THE GENTILES.
HAVE YOU INQUIRED OF THE LORD?
NO. THE LORD MAKES NO SUCH THINGS KNOWN TO US.

HOW CAN YOU NOT SIMPLY KEEP HIS COMMANDMENTS? WHY MUST YOU PERISH BECAUSE OF YOUR HARD HEARTS?
REMEMBER WHAT THE LORD HAS SAID? IF YOU WILL NOT HARDEN YOUR HEARTS, AND ASK IN FAITH, BELIEVING THAT YOU WILL RECEIVE, THESE THINGS WILL BE MADE KNOWN TO YOU.
THE HOUSE OF ISRAEL WAS COMPARED TO AN OLIVE TREE, BY THE SPIRIT OF THE LORD IN OUR FATHER. ARE WE NOT BROKEN OFF LIKE A BRANCH FROM THE HOUSE OF ISRAEL?
IN THE LATTER DAYS, AFTER OUR SEED HAS DWINDLED IN UNBELIEF, AFTER THE MESSIAH HAS COME IN BODY, THE FULNESS OF HIS GOSPEL WILL COME TO THE REMNANT OF OUR SEED WHO WILL THEN KNOW THEY ARE OF THE HOUSE OF ISRAEL--THE COVENANT PEOPLE OF THE LORD.
AT THAT DAY, WILL THEY NOT RECEIVE THE STRENGTH AND NOURISHMENT FROM THE TRUE VINE? THEY SHALL BE GRAFTED IN AS A NATURAL BRANCH OF THE OLIVE-TREE INTO THE TRUE FOLD OF GOD.
THIS IS WHAT OUR FATHER'S WORDS MEAN...
...THE LORD PROMISED OUR FATHER ABRAHAM THAT IN HIS SEED ALL THE KINDREDS OF THE EARTH WILL BE BLESSED.
AND SO I, NEPHI, SAID MANY THINGS TO THEM CONCERNING THESE THINGS AND THE RESTORATION OF THE JEWS IN THE LATTER DAYS.

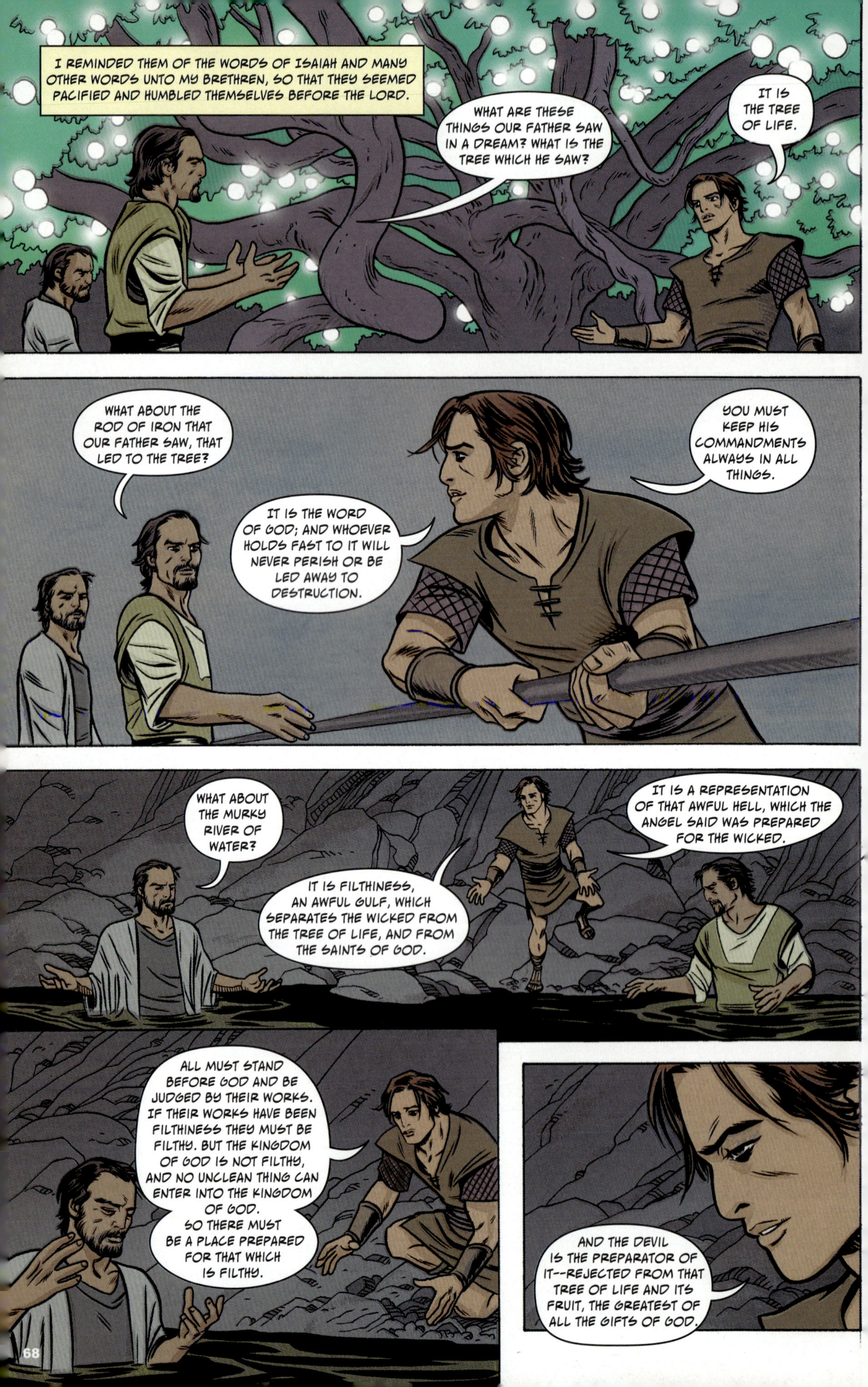
I REMINDED THEM OF THE WORDS OF ISAIAH AND MANY OTHER WORDS UNTO MY BRETHREN, SO THAT THEY SEEMED PACIFIED AND HUMBLED THEMSELVES BEFORE THE LORD.
WHAT ARE THESE THINGS OUR FATHER SAW IN A DREAM? WHAT IS THE TREE WHICH HE SAW?
IT IS THE TREE OF LIFE.
WHAT ABOUT THE ROD OF IRON THAT OUR FATHER SAW, THAT LED TO THE TREE?
IT IS THE WORD OF GOD; AND WHOEVER HOLDS FAST TO IT WILL NEVER PERISH OR BE LED AWAY TO DESTRUCTION.
YOU MUST KEEP HIS COMMANDMENTS ALWAYS IN ALL THINGS.
WHAT ABOUT THE MURKY RIVER OF WATER?
IT IS FILTHINESS, AN AWFUL GULF, WHICH SEPARATES THE WICKED FROM THE TREE OF LIFE, AND FROM THE SAINTS OF GOD.
IT IS A REPRESENTATION OF THAT AWFUL HELL, WHICH THE ANGEL SAID WAS PREPARED FOR THE WICKED.
ALL MUST STAND BEFORE GOD AND BE JUDGED BY THEIR WORKS. IF THEIR WORKS HAVE BEEN FILTHINESS THEY MUST BE FILTHY. BUT THE KINGDOM OF GOD IS NOT FILTHY, AND NO UNCLEAN THING CAN ENTER INTO THE KINGDOM OF GOD. SO THERE MUST BE A PLACE PREPARED FOR THAT WHICH IS FILTHY.
AND THE DEVIL IS THE PREPARATOR OF IT--REJECTED FROM THAT TREE OF LIFE AND ITS FRUIT, THE GREATEST OF ALL THE GIFTS OF GOD.

CHAPTER 16
YOU DECLARE MORE HARD THINGS THAT WE ARE UNABLE TO BEAR!
THE GUILTY TAKE THE TRUTH HARD BECAUSE IT CUTS TO THE VERY CENTER.
WALK UPRIGHTLY BEFORE GOD, THEN YOU WILL NOT COMPLAIN ABOUT HARD THINGS SAID AGAINST YOU.

AND IT CAME TO PASS THAT I, NEPHI, TOOK ONE OF THE DAUGHTERS OF ISHMAEL TO BE MY WIFE.
AND MY BROTHERS ALSO.
ZORAM MARRIED THE ELDEST DAUGHTER FROM THE HOUSE OF ISHMAEL.
AND SO MY FATHER, LEHI, HAD FULFILLED ALL THE COMMANDMENTS OF THE LORD WHICH HAD BEEN GIVEN UNTO HIM. AND ALSO, I, NEPHI, HAD BEEN GREATLY BLESSED OF THE LORD.

IT CAME TO PASS THAT THE VOICE OF THE LORD SPOKE TO MY FATHER BY NIGHT, AND COMMANDED HIM THAT ON THE MORROW HE SHOULD TAKE HIS JOURNEY INTO THE WILDERNESS.
AS MY FATHER AROSE IN THE MORNING HE FOUND A ROUND BALL OF CURIOUS WORKMANSHIP.
IT WAS OF FINE BRASS. AND WITHIN THE BALL WERE TWO SPINDLES.

AND ONE POINTED TOWARD WHERE WE SHOULD GO INTO THE WILDERNESS.
AND SO WE GATHERED ALL THE REMAINDER OF OUR PROVISIONS WHICH THE LORD HAD GIVEN TO US AND DEPARTED INTO THE WILDERNESS, ACROSS THE RIVER LAMAN.
AND IT CAME TO PASS THAT WE TRAVELED FOR THE SPACE OF FOUR DAYS, NEARLY A SOUTH SOUTHEAST DIRECTION, WHEN WE PITCHED OUR TENTS AGAIN, WE CALLED THE PLACE SHAZER.
RED SEA
SHAZER
AND WE TOOK OUR BOWS AND ARROWS AND OUR SLINGS AND STONES HUNTING FOOD FOR OUR FAMILIES AS WE TRAVELED ON INTO THE WILDERNESS, FOLLOWING THE DIRECTIONS OF THE BALL, KEEPING US IN THE MOST FERTILE PARTS OF THE WILDERNESS IN THE BORDERS NEAR THE RED SEA.

AND AS I, NEPHI, WENT FORTH TO SLAY FOOD...
...I BROKE MY BOW, WHICH WAS MADE OF FINE STEEL.
THAT WAS OUR BEST BOW, NEPHI! OURS HAVE LOST THEIR SPRING.
SLINGS AND STONES?! IS THAT WHAT WE ARE LEFT TO HUNT WITH? SLINGS AND STONES?!
HUNGRY AND TIRED FROM OUR TRAVELS AND WITH NO FOOD TO SUSTAIN US, IT TOOK ITS TOLL.

I SHOULD HAVE KEPT THAT BOW FOR MYSELF.
WE HAVE NO MORE ARROWS, LAMAN!
I DON'T NEED ARROWS TO TAKE THE FLESH OF THAT FOOL NEPHI.
TAKE MY FLESH. I AM THE FOOL IF YOU NEED ONE TO BLAME. I TRUSTED THE LORD. BLAME ME.
NO, FATHER! ALL OF YOU! WHERE IS YOUR FAITH?
NOT ONE MORE WORD, NEPHI! NOT ONE WORD.

FATHER, WHERE SHOULD I GO TO GET FOOD?
FORGIVE ME, MY SON.
MY FATHER HUMBLED HIMSELF AND INQUIRED OF THE LORD. AND THE VOICE OF THE LORD SAID FOR HIM TO LOOK UPON THE BALL AND SEE THE THINGS WHICH ARE WRITTEN.

MY FATHER WAS TRULY CHASTENED BECAUSE OF HIS MURMURING AGAINST THE LORD.
AND WHEN MY FATHER BEHELD THE THINGS WHICH WERE WRITTEN UPON THE BALL EVERYONE TREMBLED WITH FEAR.
THE BALL, NAMED THE LIAHONA, REVEALED A NEW WRITING, WHICH WAS PLAIN TO BE READ, GIVING US UNDERSTANDING CONCERNING THE WAYS OF THE LORD.
THE WRITING CHANGED FROM TIME TO TIME, ACCORDING TO THE FAITH AND DILIGENCE WHICH WE GAVE IT. AND SO WE SEE THAT BY SMALL MEANS THE LORD CAN BRING ABOUT GREAT THINGS.
AND SO I WENT TO THE TOP OF THE MOUNTAIN, ACCORDING TO THE DIRECTIONS GIVEN UPON THE BALL.
AND IT CAME TO PASS THAT I DID SLAY WILD BEASTS, OBTAINING FOOD FOR MY FAMILY.

AFTER TRAVELING FOR MANY DAYS IN NEARLY THE SAME COURSE AS IN THE BEGINNING, IT CAME TO PASS THAT ISHMAEL DIED.
HE WAS BURIED IN THE PLACE WE CALLED NAHOM.
OUR FATHER IS DEAD. AFTER ENDLESS WANDERING, AND SUFFERING HUNGER, THIRST, AND FATIGUE--ALL THIS ONLY TO PERISH IN THE WILDERNESS.
NO MORE! I WON'T FOLLOW YOU ANYMORE. OR YOU. NO MORE VISIONS! NO MORE TALK OF DESTRUCTION IN JERUSALEM. WE WANT YOU TO TAKE US BACK HOME.

THEN LET US SLAY OUR FATHER.
AND NEPHI, WHO HAS TAKEN IT UPON HIMSELF TO BE OUR RULER AND OUR TEACHER. WE ARE HIS ELDER BRETHREN.
HE SAYS THAT THE LORD TALKS WITH HIM, AND THAT ANGELS MINISTER TO HIM. BUT WE KNOW HE LIES TO US-- WORKING HIS CUNNING ARTS TO DECEIVE OUR EYES.
HE THINKS HE CAN LEAD US AWAY TO SOME STRANGE WORLD TO MAKE HIMSELF A KING AND A RULER OVER US-- BENDING US TO HIS WILL AND PLEASURE.
LOOK! THE LORD HAS BLESSED US WITH MORE FOOD.
CHASTENED BY THE LORD THEY TURNED AWAY THEIR ANGER.
CHAPTER 17
ABOUT 592-591 B.C.
THOUGH WE STRUGGLED WITH MANY AFFLICTIONS, OUR WOMEN BORE CHILDREN IN THE WILDERNESS. GREAT WERE THE BLESSINGS OF THE LORD UPON US. WE OFTEN LIVED ON RAW MEAT, BUT OUR WOMAN HAD PLENTY OF MILK FOR OUR CHILDREN. AND THEY WERE AS STRONG AS THE MEN WITHOUT COMPLAINING.
AND SO WE SEE THAT IF THE CHILDREN OF MEN KEEP THE COMMANDMENTS OF GOD HE NOURISHES THEM, AND STRENGTHENS THEM, AND PROVIDES THE MEANS TO ACCOMPLISH WHAT HE ASKS.
RED SEA
SHAZER
NAHOM
AND WE DID SOJOURN AS MUCH AS EIGHT YEARS IN THE WILDERNESS.

AND WE CAME TO THE LAND WHICH WE CALLED BOUNTIFUL, BECAUSE OF ALL ITS FRUIT AND WILD HONEY.
ALL THESE THINGS WERE PREPARED OF THE LORD THAT WE MIGHT NOT PERISH.
AND WE SAW THE SEA, WHICH WE CALLED IRREANTUM, BEING INTERPRETED, IS MANY WATERS.
AND WE PITCHED OUR TENTS BY THE SEASHORE.
EVEN THOUGH WE HAD SUFFERED MANY AFFLICTIONS AND DIFFICULTY, SO MUCH THAT WE CANNOT WRITE THEM ALL, WE REJOICED WHEN WE CAME TO THE PLACE BOUNTIFUL.

ARISE AND GET THEE INTO THE MOUNTAIN.
AND IT CAME TO PASS THAT I AROSE AND WENT UP INTO THE MOUNTAIN AND CRIED UNTO THE LORD.
AND THE LORD SPOKE TO ME.
CONSTRUCT A SHIP, AFTER THE MANNER WHICH I WILL SHOW YOU, SO THAT I MAY CARRY YOUR PEOPLE ACROSS THESE WATERS.
LORD, WHERE DO I FIND ORE TO MOLTEN, TO MAKE THE TOOLS TO CONSTRUCT THE SHIP YOU HAVE SHOWN ME?
AND THE LORD TOLD ME WHERE I SHOULD GO TO FIND ORE, THAT I MIGHT MAKE TOOLS.
AND I MADE A BELLOWS FROM THE SKINS OF BEASTS TO BLOW THE FIRE WHICH I MADE FROM STRIKING TWO STONES.
WE HAVE NOT MADE MUCH FIRE AS WE JOURNEYED. BUT THE LORD HAS MADE OUR FOOD SWEET WHEN WE DID NOT COOK IT.
HE HAD TOLD US HE WOULD BE OUR LIGHT IN THE WILDERNESS, PREPARING THE WAY FOR US TO THE PROMISED LAND, AS LONG AS WE KEPT HIS COMMANDMENTS.

A SHIP?!
IS THIS NOT THE PROMISED LAND?
OUR BROTHER IS A FOOL! HE THINKS HE CAN BUILD A SHIP!
YOU THINK WE CAN CROSS THESE GREAT WATERS?!
WELL, I WILL NOT HELP YOU IN THIS INSANE TASK!
IF IT CAN BE DONE, YOU CAN DO IT ALONE! YOU AND YOUR LORD!
I DO NEED YOUR HELP. AND IT CAN BE DONE.
BUT IT WILL NOT BE DONE. YOU LACK JUDGEMENT, NEPHI! NOT EVEN YOU CAN ACCOMPLISH SO GREAT A WORK.
STOP BEING LIKE OUR FATHER WITH HIS FOOLISH IMAGINATIONS. LOOK AT THE SUFFERING OF OUR WOMEN.
IT WOULD HAVE BEEN BETTER THAT THEY HAD DIED BEFORE THEY CAME OUT OF JERUSALEM THAN TO SUFFER ALL THESE AFFLICTIONS
ALL THESE YEARS WE COULD HAVE ENJOYED OUR POSSESSIONS AND THE LAND OF OUR INHERITANCE. WE MIGHT HAVE BEEN HAPPY.
THERE WAS NO DESTRUCTION. NO. EVERY STEP OF THE WAY WE HAVE TRIED TO FIND REASON IN YOU AND YET WE CARRIED ON THIS PATH OF FOLLY.
DO YOU BELIEVE THAT OUR FATHERS, THE CHILDREN OF ISRAEL, WOULD HAVE BEEN FREED FROM THE EGYPTIANS IF THEY DID NOT LISTEN TO THE WORDS OF THE LORD?

YOU KNOW THAT MOSES WAS COMMANDED OF THE LORD TO DO THAT GREAT WORK AND BY HIS WORD THE WATERS OF THE RED SEA WERE DIVIDED SO THEY COULD PASS THROUGH ON DRY GROUND.
AND THE THE ARMIES OF PHARAOH WERE DROWNED IN THE SEA IN PURSUIT.
BUT EVEN THOUGH FREED FROM BONDAGE AND GIVEN MANNA FROM HEAVEN AND WATER FROM STONE, WITH HARDENED HEARTS THEY STILL REVILED AGAINST MOSES AND THE TRUE LIVING GOD.
AND JUST LIKE MOSES, THE LORD COMMANDED MY FATHER THAT HE SHOULD DEPART INTO THE WILDERNESS.
YOU HAVE SEEN AN ANGEL. AND HE HAS SPOKEN TO YOU IN A STILL SMALL VOICE, BUT YOU WERE PAST FEELING, THAT YOU COULD NOT FEEL HIS WORDS.
AND YOU ARE SWIFT TO DO INIQUITY BUT SLOW TO REMEMBER THE LORD YOUR GOD.
YOU SHOULD KNOW THAT BY THE POWER OF HIS ALMIGHTY WORD HE CAN CAUSE THE EARTH TO PASS AWAY. OR TO CAUSE ROUGH PLACES TO BE MADE SMOOTH, AND SMOOTH PLACES BROKEN UP.
O, THEN, WHY IS IT, THAT YOU CAN STILL BE SO HARD IN YOUR HEARTS?
BEHOLD, MY SOUL IS RENT WITH ANGUISH BECAUSE OF YOU. I FEAR YOU SHALL BE CAST OFF FOREVER.
I AM FULL OF THE SPIRIT OF GOD, SO MUCH THAT MY FRAME HAS NO STRENGTH.

LET US RELEASE YOU FROM YOUR PAIN, NEPHI.
YES. LET US THROW HIM IN THE SEA.
A BRIEF MOMENT OF PAIN AS YOUR BODY IS CRUSHED AGAINST ROCK AND LUNGS BURST FROM DROWNING.
BUT THEN ETERNAL PEACE SHALL BE YOURS IN THE DEPTHS OF THE SEA, NEPHI.
IN THE NAME OF THE ALMIGHTY GOD, I COMMAND THAT YOU NOT TOUCH ME, FOR I AM FILLED WITH THE POWER OF GOD, EVEN UNTO THE CONSUMING OF MY FLESH.
ANYONE WHO LAYS THEIR HANDS ON ME SHALL WITHER LIKE A DRIED REED.
WE WILL BUILD A SHIP FOR GOD HAS COMMANDED IT. YOU WILL NOT HOLD YOUR LABOR FROM ME AND YOU WILL NOT COMPLAIN AGAINST FATHER ANYMORE.

NEPHI.
GO AND STRETCH FORTH YOUR HAND AGAIN TO YOUR BRETHREN, AND THEY WILL NOT WITHER BEFORE YOU, BUT I WILL SHOCK THEM, AND THIS I WILL DO, THAT THEY MAY KNOW THAT I AM THE LORD THEIR GOD.
BROTHERS, IT IS TIME TO BEGIN OUR LABORS.
NEPHI GO **REST** YOURSELF. WE WILL HEAR **NOTHING** FROM YOU TODAY.

WE KNOW OF A SURETY THAT THE LORD IS WITH YOU.
WE KNOW THAT IT IS THE POWER OF THE LORD THAT HAS SHAKEN US.
WE WILL DO AS YOU SAY. COMMAND US AND WE WILL WORSHIP AND FOLLOW YOU.
NO. I AM YOUR BROTHER, EVEN YOUR YOUNGER BROTHER.
WORSHIP THE LORD YOUR GOD, AND HONOR YOUR FATHER AND YOUR MOTHER, THAT YOUR DAYS MAY BE LONG IN THE LAND WHICH GOD SHALL GIVE YOU.
CHAPTER 18
THEN THEY DID WORSHIP THE LORD, AND WENT WITH ME, CRAFTING TIMBERS OF CURIOUS WORKMANSHIP. AND THE LORD DID SHOW ME FROM TIME TO TIME THE WAY I SHOULD BUILD THE SHIP.

AND SO I, NEPHI, DID NOT WORK THE TIMBERS IN WAYS LEARNED BY MEN. BUT BUILT IT AFTER THE MANNER WHICH THE LORD HAD SHOWN TO ME.
I WENT TO THE MOUNTAIN OFTEN AND PRAYED. AND THE LORD SHOWED ME GREAT THINGS.
IT IS FINE. VERY FINE.
LET US GIVE THANKS TO THE LORD.
WE MUST ARISE AND GO DOWN INTO THE SHIP. WE MUST PREPARE ALL THINGS.
WE MUST LOAD THE SHIP WITH FRUITS, MEAT, SEEDS, HONEY, AND ALL THE PROVISIONS ACCORDING TO WHAT THE LORD HAS COMMANDED.

AND NOW, MY FATHER HAD BEGAT TWO SONS IN THE WILDERNESS, JACOB, AND MY YOUNGEST BROTHER, JOSEPH.
AND IT CAME TO PASS WE TOOK TO THE SEA AND WERE DRIVEN BY THE WIND TOWARDS THE PROMISED LAND.

NEPHI, BRING US MORE FOOD AND DRINK, AND THEN HIDE YOURSELF FROM US. I DON'T WANT TO SMELL YOU THIS DAY.
BRETHREN, THERE IS WORK TO BE DONE. OUR COURSE MUST BE KEPT.
JACOB, CAN YOU PLEASE BRING ME THE LIAHONA?
THE IGNORANT FOOL NEVER CEASES TO RULE EVERY BREATH AND MOMENT.
I WON'T BE WORKING THIS DAY. BABY JOSEPH SHOULD START PULLING HIS SHARE.
DUMB SAM AND OLD LEHI CAN FILL THE GAP IN YOUR LABORS AS WELL.
THANK YOU, JACOB. CAN YOU HOLD IT A WHILE LONGER FOR ME?
THERE ARE LABORS THAT CAN NOT WAIT. YOU KNOW THAT SAM AND THE OTHERS KEPT WATCH THROUGH THE NIGHT AND I WILL NOT DISRESPECT OUR FATHER WHO CAN BARELY LEAVE HIS BED.
AND YOU LAUGH.

MIND YOUR PLACE!
I WEARY HOW OUR YOUNGER BROTHER ACTS AS **RULER** OVER US!
LET US TEST OUR TYING SKILLS AGAIN. I DO NOT THINK I DID MY BEST BEFORE.
DO NOT DO THIS, LEMUEL!
YOU NEED TO REST YOUR BURDENS EVEN IF WE MUST FORCE YOU TO DO SO.
WE WILL TAKE THE HELM AND LEAD THE WAY FOR NOW.
GIVE ME THE BALL, BOY!
DID YOU BREAK IT? IT NO LONGER SEEMS TO WORK.
NO MATTER. THE WIND STILL CARRIES US. LET IT.
WHAT ARE YOU **DOING?** IS THIS A NEW GAME? WILL YOU **NEVER** LEARN WHAT YOU HAVE BEEN TAUGHT SO OFTEN?!

LAMAN! A TEMPEST ON THE HORIZON!
A GREAT AND TERRIBLE TEMPEST, AND WE WERE DRIVEN BACK UPON THE WATERS FOR THE SPACE OF THREE DAYS.
AND THEY BEGAN TO BE FRIGHTENED, TERRIFIED THAT THEY WOULD BE DROWNED IN THE SEA.
SET MY HUSBAND LOOSE! YOU WILL SURELY KILL US ALL!
PLEASE STAY WITH THE OTHERS! HOLD TO YOUR FAITH!

NEVERTHELESS THEY DID NOT LOOSE ME.
I WILL KILL ANYONE WHO EVEN SPEAKS OF LOOSING NEPHI.
AND ON THE FOURTH DAY, THE TEMPEST BEGAN TO BE EVEN WORSE AND WE WERE ABOUT TO BE SWALLOWED UP IN THE DEPTHS OF THE SEA.
THE JUDGEMENTS OF GOD ARE UPON US! GIVE THE SHIP TO NEPHI!
WE MUST REPENT, LAMAN!
NO!

VERY WELL...
...SAVE US THEN IF YOU CAN.
SAVE US NEPHI!

THEN YOU ARE NOT PAST LEARNING?
BECAUSE OF THEIR GRIEF AND MUCH SORROW, MY PARENTS WERE ABOUT TO BE CAST WITH SORROW INTO A WATERY GRAVE.
MY WIFE WITH HER TEARS AND PRAYERS, AND ALSO MY CHILDREN, DID NOT SOFTEN THE HEARTS OF MY BRETHREN THAT THEY WOULD LOOSE ME.
THERE WAS NOTHING EXCEPT THE POWER OF GOD, WHICH THREATENED THEM WITH DESTRUCTION, THAT COULD SOFTEN THEIR HEARTS.
ONLY WHEN THEY SAW THEY WERE ABOUT TO BE SWALLOWED UP IN THE DEPTHS OF THE SEA WOULD THEY REPENT, AND FINALLY CUT ME LOOSE.
AFTER THEY HAD FREED ME, I TOOK THE COMPASS, AND IT WORKED HOW I DESIRED. I PRAYED TO THE LORD AND THE WINDS AND THE STORM CEASED, BRINGING A GREAT CALM.
AND SO, WITH GOD'S BLESSINGS, I, NEPHI, DID GUIDE THE SHIP.
AND WE SAILED AGAIN TOWARDS THE PROMISED LAND.

AND IT CAME TO PASS THAT AFTER WE HAD SAILED FOR THE SPACE OF MANY DAYS WE DID ARRIVE AT THE PROMISED LAND.
IS THAT IT, NEPHI?
IS IT THE PROMISED LAND, FATHER?
YES. THIS IS THE PROMISED LAND WHICH THE LORD OUR GOD HAS PREPARED FOR US.

The Promised Land

AND WE WENT FORTH UPON THE LAND...
...AND WE PITCHED OUR TENTS.

AND SOON WE BEGAN TO TILL THE EARTH, AND WE BEGAN TO PLANT ALL OUR SEEDS INTO THE EARTH, WHICH WE HAD BROUGHT FROM THE LAND OF JERUSALEM.
AND THEY GREW AND WE WERE BLESSED IN ABUNDANCE.
AND IT CAME TO PASS THAT WE FOUND MANY THINGS IN THE LAND OF PROMISE, AS WE JOURNEYED IN ITS WILDERNESS.
THERE WERE BEASTS IN THE FORESTS OF EVERY KIND, BOTH THE COW, THE OX, THE ASS AND THE HORSE. THERE WERE GOATS, AND ALL MANNER OF WILD ANIMALS, WHICH WERE FOR THE USE OF MEN.
AND WE DID FIND ALL MANNER OF ORE. GOLD, SILVER, AND COPPER.
CHAPTER 19
BETWEEN 588 AND 570 B.C.
AND IT CAME TO PASS THAT THE LORD COMMANDED ME TO MAKE PLATES OF ORE TO ENGRAVE A HISTORY OF MY PEOPLE, OUR JOURNEYINGS, MY FATHER'S PROPHECIES AND EVEN MY OWN.
THE MORE PLAIN AND PRECIOUS PARTS OF THE MINISTRIES AND PROPHECIES SHOULD BE WRITTEN ON THESE PLATES FOR THE INSTRUCTION OF MY PEOPLE, AND FOR OTHER WISE PURPOSES KNOWN ONLY TO THE LORD.

WHEREFORE, I, NEPHI, DID MAKE A RECORD ON THE OTHER PLATES WHICH GIVES A GREATER ACCOUNT OF THE WARS AND CONTENTIONS AND DESTRUCTIONS OF MY PEOPLE. AND THESE PLATES SHOULD BE HANDED DOWN FROM ONE GENERATION TO ANOTHER, OR FROM ONE PROPHET TO ANOTHER, UNTIL THE LORD COMMANDS US FURTHER.
IF I ERR, OR THOSE OF OLD, I WOULD NOT EXCUSE MYSELF BECAUSE OF OTHERS, BUT ONLY BECAUSE OF MY OWN WEAKNESS, WOULD EXCUSE MYSELF.
FOR THE THINGS WHICH SOME MEN FEEL ARE OF GREAT WORTH, OTHERS TRAMPLE UNDER THEIR FEET. EVEN THE VERY GOD OF ISRAEL DO MEN TRAMPLE UNDER THEIR FEET.
AND HE WILL COME, ACCORDING TO THE WORDS OF THE ANGEL, IN SIX HUNDRED YEARS FROM THE TIME MY FATHER LEFT JERUSALEM.
AND THE WORLD, BECAUSE OF THEIR INIQUITY, WILL SCOURGE AND SMITE HIM, AND HE WILL SUFFER IT BECAUSE OF HIS LOVING KINDNESS AND LONG-SUFFERING TOWARDS THE CHILDREN OF MEN.
AND THE GOD OF OUR FATHERS WILL GIVE HIMSELF, AS A MAN, INTO THE HANDS OF WICKED MEN, TO BE LIFTED UP, ACCORDING TO THE WORDS OF ZENOCK, AND TO BE CRUCIFIED, ACCORDING TO THE WORDS OF NEUM, AND TO BE BURIED IN A SEPULCHRE, ACCORDING TO THE WORDS OF ZENOS, AND THE THREE DAYS OF DARKNESS, WHICH WILL BE A SIGN OF HIS DEATH AROUND THE WORLD.
THE LORD GOD SURELY SHALL VISIT ALL THE HOUSE OF ISRAEL AT THAT DAY, SOME WITH HIS VOICE AND GREAT JOY...
...OTHERS WITH THUNDERINGS, LIGHTNINGS, TEMPEST, FIRE, SMOKE, AND VAPOR OF DARKNESS, AND BY THE OPENING OF THE EARTH.
MANY WILL EXCLAIM: THE GOD OF NATURE SUFFERS.

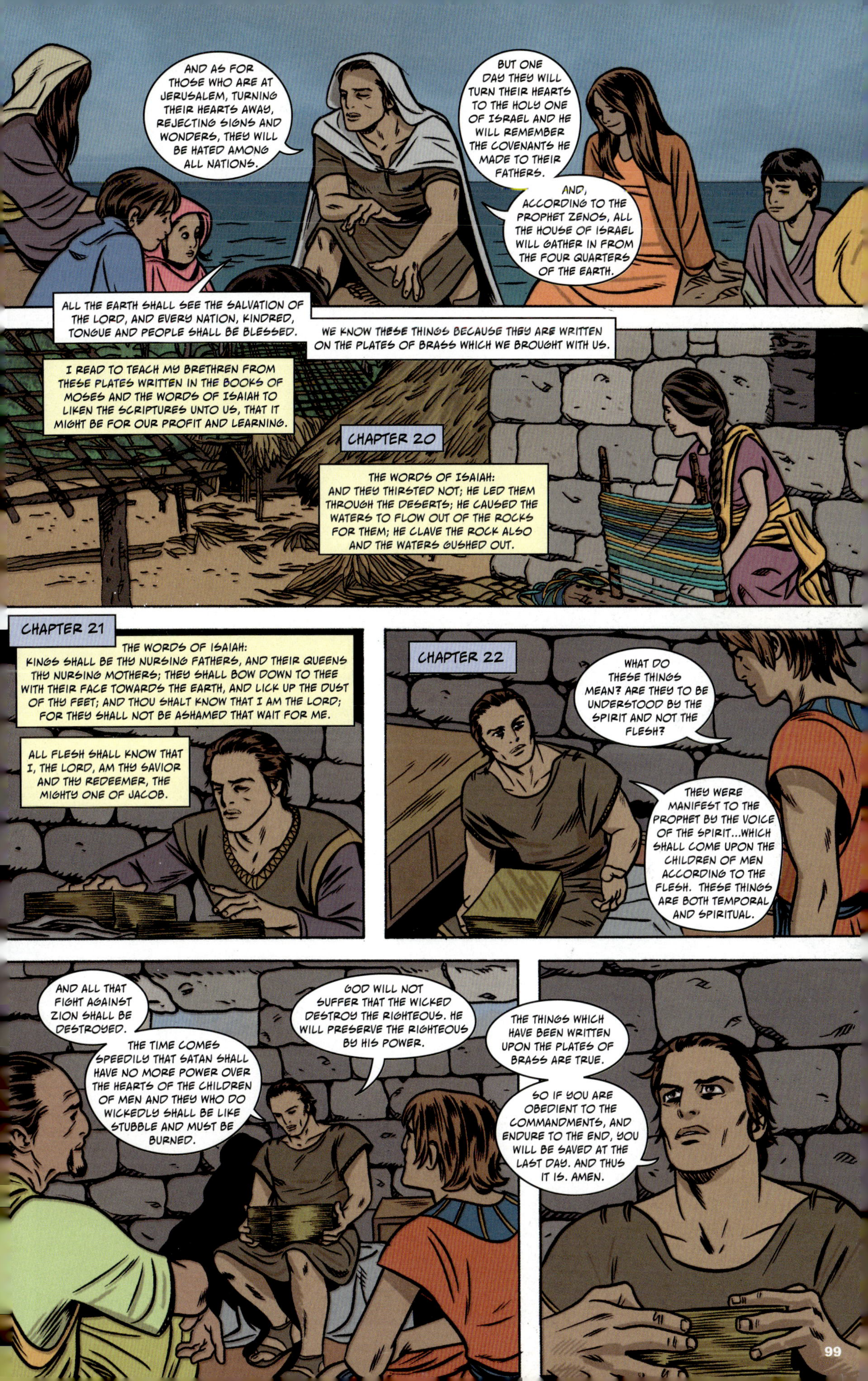

AND AS FOR THOSE WHO ARE AT JERUSALEM, TURNING THEIR HEARTS AWAY, REJECTING SIGNS AND WONDERS, THEY WILL BE HATED AMONG ALL NATIONS.
BUT ONE DAY THEY WILL TURN THEIR HEARTS TO THE HOLY ONE OF ISRAEL AND HE WILL REMEMBER THE COVENANTS HE MADE TO THEIR FATHERS.
AND, ACCORDING TO THE PROPHET ZENOS, ALL THE HOUSE OF ISRAEL WILL GATHER IN FROM THE FOUR QUARTERS OF THE EARTH.
ALL THE EARTH SHALL SEE THE SALVATION OF THE LORD, AND EVERY NATION, KINDRED, TONGUE AND PEOPLE SHALL BE BLESSED.
WE KNOW THESE THINGS BECAUSE THEY ARE WRITTEN ON THE PLATES OF BRASS WHICH WE BROUGHT WITH US.
I READ TO TEACH MY BRETHREN FROM THESE PLATES WRITTEN IN THE BOOKS OF MOSES AND THE WORDS OF ISAIAH TO LIKEN THE SCRIPTURES UNTO US, THAT IT MIGHT BE FOR OUR PROFIT AND LEARNING.
CHAPTER 20
THE WORDS OF ISAIAH: AND THEY THIRSTED NOT; HE LED THEM THROUGH THE DESERTS; HE CAUSED THE WATERS TO FLOW OUT OF THE ROCKS FOR THEM; HE CLAVE THE ROCK ALSO AND THE WATERS GUSHED OUT.
CHAPTER 21
THE WORDS OF ISAIAH: KINGS SHALL BE THY NURSING FATHERS, AND THEIR QUEENS THY NURSING MOTHERS; THEY SHALL BOW DOWN TO THEE WITH THEIR FACE TOWARDS THE EARTH, AND LICK UP THE DUST OF THY FEET; AND THOU SHALT KNOW THAT I AM THE LORD; FOR THEY SHALL NOT BE ASHAMED THAT WAIT FOR ME.
ALL FLESH SHALL KNOW THAT I, THE LORD, AM THY SAVIOR AND THY REDEEMER, THE MIGHTY ONE OF JACOB.
CHAPTER 22
WHAT DO THESE THINGS MEAN? ARE THEY TO BE UNDERSTOOD BY THE SPIRIT AND NOT THE FLESH?
THEY WERE MANIFEST TO THE PROPHET BY THE VOICE OF THE SPIRIT...WHICH SHALL COME UPON THE CHILDREN OF MEN ACCORDING TO THE FLESH. THESE THINGS ARE BOTH TEMPORAL AND SPIRITUAL.
AND ALL THAT FIGHT AGAINST ZION SHALL BE DESTROYED.
THE TIME COMES SPEEDILY THAT SATAN SHALL HAVE NO MORE POWER OVER THE HEARTS OF THE CHILDREN OF MEN AND THEY WHO DO WICKEDLY SHALL BE LIKE STUBBLE AND MUST BE BURNED.
GOD WILL NOT SUFFER THAT THE WICKED DESTROY THE RIGHTEOUS. HE WILL PRESERVE THE RIGHTEOUS BY HIS POWER.
THE THINGS WHICH HAVE BEEN WRITTEN UPON THE PLATES OF BRASS ARE TRUE.
SO IF YOU ARE OBEDIENT TO THE COMMANDMENTS, AND ENDURE TO THE END, YOU WILL BE SAVED AT THE LAST DAY. AND THUS IT IS. AMEN.

THE SECOND BOOK OF NEPHI
CHAPTER 1
BETWEEN 588 AND 570 B.C.
HOW GREAT ARE THE THINGS WHICH GOD HAS DONE FOR US BRINGING US OUT OF JERUSALEM TO THIS BEAUTIFUL LAND OF PROMISE.
HOW SAD ARE OUR REBELLIONS.
HOW GREAT IS THE LORD'S FORGIVENESS.
I HAVE SEEN A VISION, IN WHICH I KNOW THAT JERUSALEM IS DESTROYED.
WE HAVE OBTAINED A LAND OF PROMISE, CHOICE ABOVE ALL OTHER LANDS. THE LORD HAS COVENANTED THIS LAND TO ME, AND MY CHILDREN FOREVER, AND ALSO TO ALL THOSE LED OUT OF OTHER COUNTRIES BY THE HAND OF THE LORD.
IT SHALL BE A LAND OF LIBERTY TO THEM. AND IF THEY KEEP HIS COMMANDMENTS THEY WILL DWELL SAFELY FOREVER.

BUT BEHOLD, WHEN THEY DWINDLE IN UNBELIEF, HE WILL BRING OTHER NATIONS UNTO THEM GIVING THEM POWER...
...AND HE WILL TAKE AWAY THE LANDS OF THEIR POSSESSIONS, AND THEY WILL BE SCATTERED AND SMITTEN.
HEAR THE WORDS OF A TREMBLING PARENT WHO SOON MUST GO THE WAY OF ALL THE EARTH.
I DO NOT FEAR FOR MYSELF. I AM ENCIRCLED ABOUT ETERNALLY IN THE ARMS OF GOD'S LOVE.
I FEAR FOR THE HARDENING OF MY CHILDREN'S HEARTS THAT YOU WOULD BE CUT OFF AND DESTROYED FOREVER.
OR THAT A CURSING SHOULD COME UPON YOU FOR THE SPACE OF MANY GENERATIONS, LED ACCORDING TO THE WILL OF THE DEVIL.
AND NOW THAT MY SOUL MIGHT HAVE JOY IN YOU, AND THAT MY HEART MIGHT LEAVE THIS WORLD WITH GLADNESS, AWAKE AND PUT ON THE ARMOR OF RIGHTEOUSNESS.
REBEL NO MORE AGAINST YOUR BROTHER, WHOSE VIEWS HAVE BEEN GLORIOUS AND AN INSTRUMENT IN THE HANDS OF GOD. WERE IT NOT FOR HIM, WE MUST HAVE PERISHED.
YOU HAVE ACCUSED HIM THAT HE SOUGHT POWER AND AUTHORITY OVER YOU; BUT I KNOW THAT HE HAS NOT. HE HAS SOUGHT THE GLORY OF GOD, AND YOUR OWN ETERNAL WELFARE.
LISTEN TO NEPHI AND I LEAVE UNTO YOU MY FIRST BLESSING.

AND NOW, ZORAM, I SPEAK UNTO YOU.
YOU WERE THE SERVANT OF LABAN, YET YOU WERE BROUGHT OUT OF THE LAND OF JERUSALEM, AND I KNOW THAT YOU ARE A TRUE FRIEND TO MY SON, NEPHI, FOREVER.
BECAUSE YOU HAVE BEEN FAITHFUL YOUR SEED WILL BE BLESSED WITH HIS SEED.
CHAPTER 2
AND NOW, JACOB, I SPEAK UNTO YOU. YOU ARE MY FIRST BORN IN THE WILDERNESS. YOU HAVE SUFFERED MUCH BECAUSE OF THE RUDENESS OF YOUR BRETHREN. NEVERTHELESS, YOU KNOW THE GREATNESS OF GOD AND YOUR SOUL SHALL BE BLESSED, AND YOU SHALL DWELL SAFELY WITH YOUR BROTHER, NEPHI. I KNOW THAT YOU ARE REDEEMED.
YOU HAVE BEHELD IN YOUR YOUTH HIS GLORY; WHEREFORE, THOU ART BLESSED EVEN AS THEY UNTO WHOM HE SHALL MINISTER IN THE FLESH; FOR THE SPIRIT IS THE SAME, YESTERDAY, TODAY, AND FOREVER. AND THE WAY IS PREPARED FROM THE FALL OF MAN, AND SALVATION IS FREE.
IT MUST BE, THAT THERE IS AN OPPOSITION IN ALL THINGS. IF NOT SO, MY FIRST-BORN IN THE WILDERNESS, RIGHTEOUSNESS COULD NOT BE BROUGHT TO PASS, NEITHER WICKEDNESS, NEITHER HOLINESS NOR MISERY, NEITHER GOOD NOR BAD. WHEREFORE, ALL THINGS MUST BE A COMPOUND IN ONE.
AND NOW, MY SONS, I SAY THESE THINGS FOR YOUR PROFIT AND LEARNING BECAUSE THERE IS A GOD...
... AND HE HAS CREATED ALL THINGS, BOTH THE HEAVENS AND THE EARTH, AND ALL THINGS THAT IN THEM ARE, BOTH THINGS TO ACT AND THINGS TO BE ACTED UPON.

IT MUST BE THAT THERE WAS AN OPPOSITION; EVEN THE FORBIDDEN FRUIT IN OPPOSITION TO THE TREE OF LIFE; THE ONE BEING SWEET AND THE OTHER BITTER.
WHEREFORE, THE LORD GOD GAVE TO MAN THAT HE SHOULD ACT FOR HIMSELF, BUT MAN COULD NOT ACT FOR HIMSELF UNLESS HE KNEW OF BOTH GOOD AND EVIL.
AND I, LEHI, ACCORDING TO THE THINGS WHICH I HAVE READ, MUST SUPPOSE THAT AN ANGEL OF GOD, ACCORDING TO WHAT IS WRITTEN, FELL FROM HEAVEN AND BECAME A DEVIL, HAVING SOUGHT WHAT WAS EVIL BEFORE GOD.
AND BECAUSE HE HAD FALLEN FROM HEAVEN TO BECOME MISERABLE FOREVER, HE HAS SOUGHT THE MISERY OF ALL MANKIND.
WHEREFORE, THE DEVIL, THE FATHER OF ALL LIES, SAID TO EVE:
PARTAKE OF THE FORBIDDEN FRUIT, AND YOU WILL NOT DIE, BUT WILL BE LIKE GOD, KNOWING GOOD AND EVIL.
AND AFTER ADAM AND EVE HAD PARTAKEN OF THE FORBIDDEN FRUIT THEY WERE DRIVEN OUT OF THE GARDEN OF EDEN, TO TILL THE EARTH.
AND THEY HAVE BROUGHT FORTH CHILDREN, THE FAMILY OF ALL THE EARTH.
AND THE DAYS OF THE CHILDREN OF MEN WERE PROLONGED THAT THEY MIGHT REPENT WHILE IN THE FLESH, A STATE OF PROBATION.
THE LORD GOD SHOWED ALL MEN WERE SUBJECT TO DEATH BECAUSE OF THE TRANSGRESSION OF THEIR PARENTS.
BUT IF ADAM HAD NOT TRANSGRESSED HE WOULD NOT HAVE FALLEN, REMAINING IN THE GARDEN OF EDEN IN THE SAME STATE FOREVER, HAVING NO END.
AND THEY WOULD HAVE HAD NO CHILDREN, REMAINING IN A STATE OF INNOCENCE, HAVING NO JOY, BECAUSE THEY KNEW NO MISERY; DOING NO GOOD, BECAUSE THEY KNEW NO SIN.
BUT BEHOLD, ALL THINGS HAVE BEEN DONE IN THE WISDOM OF HIM WHO KNOWS ALL THINGS.

ADAM FELL THAT MEN MIGHT BE; AND MEN ARE, THAT THEY MIGHT HAVE JOY.
AND THE MESSIAH WILL COME IN THE FULNESS OF TIMES, THAT HE MAY REDEEM THE CHILDREN OF MEN FROM THE FALL.
AND REDEEMED FROM THE FALL THEY ARE FREE FOREVER, KNOWING GOOD FROM EVIL AND FREE TO ACT FOR THEMSELVES AND NOT TO BE ACTED UPON, EXCEPT BY THE PUNISHMENT OF THE LAW AT THE GREAT AND LAST DAY, ACCORDING TO THE COMMANDMENTS WHICH GOD HAS GIVEN.
MEN ARE FREE TO CHOOSE LIBERTY AND ETERNAL LIFE, THROUGH THE GREAT MEDIATOR OF ALL MEN, OR TO CHOOSE CAPTIVITY AND DEATH, ACCORDING TO THE CAPTIVITY AND POWER OF THE DEVIL, WHO SEEKS THAT ALL MEN MIGHT BE MISERABLE LIKE HIMSELF.
SO, LOOK TO THE GREAT MEDIATOR, AND KEEP HIS GREAT COMMANDMENTS. BE FAITHFUL TO HIS WORDS, AND CHOOSE ETERNAL LIFE, FOLLOWING HIS HOLY SPIRIT
DO NOT CHOOSE ETERNAL DEATH, ACCORDING TO THE WILL OF THE FLESH, WHICH GIVES THE SPIRIT OF THE DEVIL POWER TO CAPTIVATE AND BRING YOU DOWN TO HELL, REIGNING OVER YOU IN HIS OWN KINGDOM.
THESE ARE THE LAST DAYS OF MY PROBATION AND I SAY THESE WORDS FOR NO OTHER REASON EXCEPT FOR THE EVERLASTING WELFARE OF YOUR SOULS. AMEN.
CHAPTER 3
AND NOW I SPEAK TO YOU, JOSEPH, MY LAST BORN.
YOUR MOTHER BORE YOU IN THE DAYS OF MY GREATEST SORROW.
AND MAY THE LORD CONSECRATE THIS LAND TO YOU, ALSO.
FOR BEHOLD, THOU ART THE FRUIT OF MY LOINS; AND I AM A DESCENDANT OF JOSEPH WHO WAS CARRIED CAPTIVE INTO EGYPT. AND GREAT WERE THE COVENANTS OF THE LORD WHICH HE MADE UNTO JOSEPH.
WHEREFORE, JOSEPH TRULY SAW OUR DAY.
YEA, JOSEPH TRULY SAID:
THUS SAITH THE LORD UNTO ME: MOSES WILL I RAISE UP, TO DELIVER THY PEOPLE OUT OF THE LAND OF EGYPT.

BUT A SEER WILL I RAISE UP OUT OF THE FRUIT OF THY LOINS; AND UNTO HIM WILL I GIVE POWER TO BRING FORTH MY WORD UNTO THE SEED OF THY LOINS...
...AND NOT TO THE BRINGING FORTH MY WORD ONLY, SAITH THE LORD, BUT TO THE CONVINCING THEM OF MY WORD, WHICH SHALL HAVE ALREADY GONE FORTH AMONG THEM.
AND BRINGING THEM TO THE KNOWLEDGE OF THEIR FATHERS IN THE LATTER DAYS, AND ALSO TO THE KNOWLEDGE OF MY COVENANTS, SAITH THE LORD.
AND OUT OF WEAKNESS HE SHALL BE MADE STRONG, IN THAT DAY WHEN MY WORK SHALL COMMENCE AMONG ALL MY PEOPLE, UNTO THE RESTORING THEE, O HOUSE OF ISRAEL, SAITH THE LORD.
BEHOLD, THAT SEER WILL THE LORD BLESS; AND THEY THAT SEEK TO DESTROY HIM SHALL BE CONFOUNDED; FOR THIS PROMISE, WHICH I HAVE OBTAINED OF THE LORD SHALL BE FULFILLED. BEHOLD, I AM SURE OF THE FULFILLING OF THIS PROMISE...
...AND HIS NAME SHALL BE CALLED AFTER ME; AND IT SHALL BE AFTER THE NAME OF HIS FATHER. AND HE SHALL BE LIKE UNTO ME; FOR THE THING, WHICH THE LORD SHALL BRING FORTH BY HIS HAND, BY THE POWER OF THE LORD SHALL BRING MY PEOPLE UNTO SALVATION.
AND NOW, BEHOLD, MY SON JOSEPH, AFTER THIS MANNER DID MY FATHER OF OLD PROPHESY. BECAUSE OF THIS COVENANT YOU ARE BLESSED; FOR YOUR SEED SHALL NOT BE DESTROYED, FOR THEY SHALL HEARKEN UNTO THE WORDS OF THE BOOK.
AND NOW, YOU ARE BLESSED, JOSEPH. BEHOLD, YOU ARE LITTLE, SO HEARKEN UNTO THE WORDS OF YOUR BROTHER, NEPHI, AND IT SHALL BE DONE ACCORDING TO THE WORDS WHICH I HAVE SPOKEN. REMEMBER THE WORDS OF YOUR DYING FATHER. AMEN.

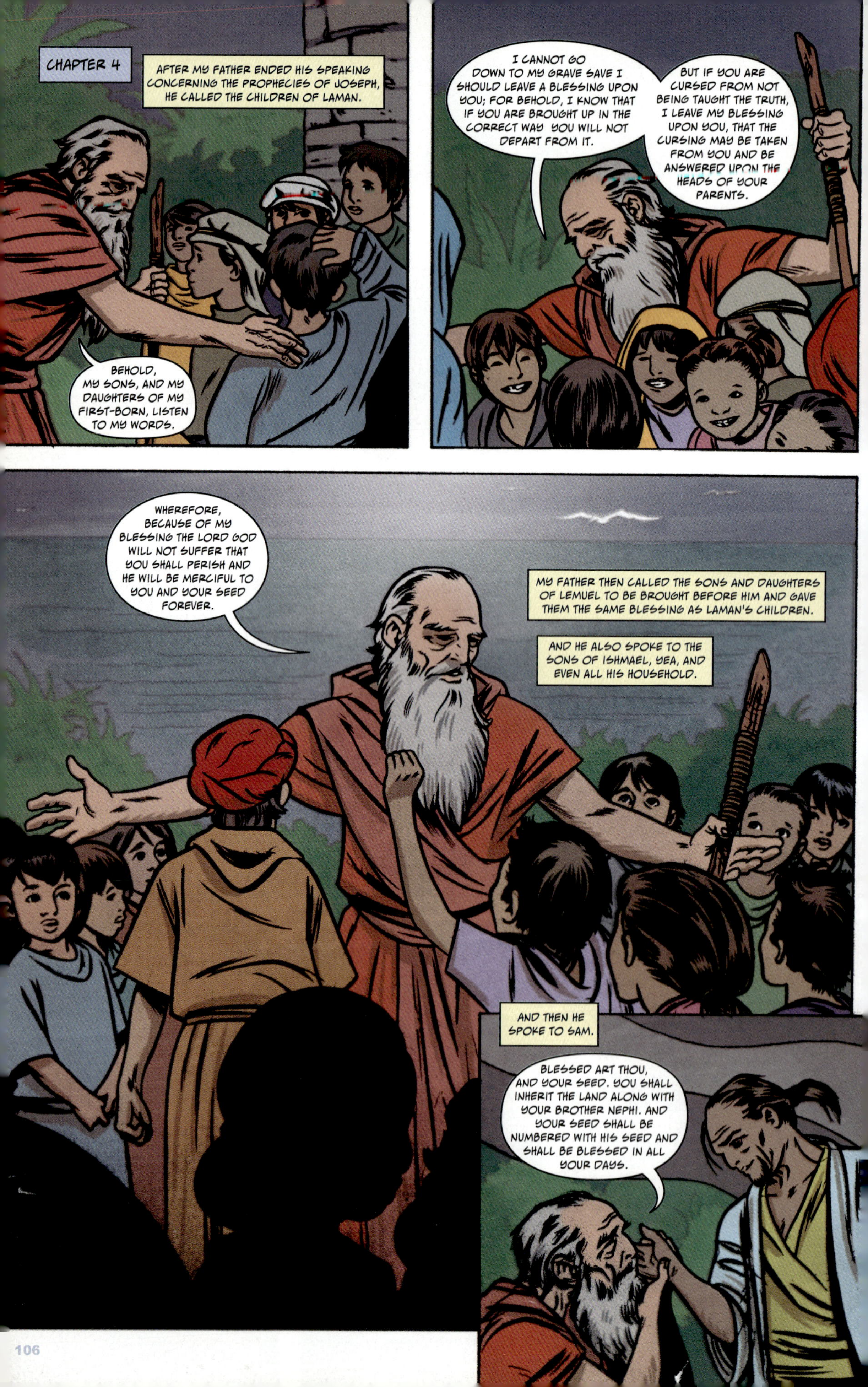
CHAPTER 4
AFTER MY FATHER ENDED HIS SPEAKING CONCERNING THE PROPHECIES OF JOSEPH, HE CALLED THE CHILDREN OF LAMAN.
BEHOLD, MY SONS, AND MY DAUGHTERS OF MY FIRST-BORN, LISTEN TO MY WORDS.
I CANNOT GO DOWN TO MY GRAVE SAVE I SHOULD LEAVE A BLESSING UPON YOU; FOR BEHOLD, I KNOW THAT IF YOU ARE BROUGHT UP IN THE CORRECT WAY YOU WILL NOT DEPART FROM IT.
BUT IF YOU ARE CURSED FROM NOT BEING TAUGHT THE TRUTH, I LEAVE MY BLESSING UPON YOU, THAT THE CURSING MAY BE TAKEN FROM YOU AND BE ANSWERED UPON THE HEADS OF YOUR PARENTS.
WHEREFORE, BECAUSE OF MY BLESSING THE LORD GOD WILL NOT SUFFER THAT YOU SHALL PERISH AND HE WILL BE MERCIFUL TO YOU AND YOUR SEED FOREVER.
MY FATHER THEN CALLED THE SONS AND DAUGHTERS OF LEMUEL TO BE BROUGHT BEFORE HIM AND GAVE THEM THE SAME BLESSING AS LAMAN'S CHILDREN.
AND HE ALSO SPOKE TO THE SONS OF ISHMAEL, YEA, AND EVEN ALL HIS HOUSEHOLD.
AND THEN HE SPOKE TO SAM.
BLESSED ART THOU, AND YOUR SEED. YOU SHALL INHERIT THE LAND ALONG WITH YOUR BROTHER NEPHI. AND YOUR SEED SHALL BE NUMBERED WITH HIS SEED AND SHALL BE BLESSED IN ALL YOUR DAYS.

AND AFTER MY FATHER, LEHI, HAD SPOKEN UNTO ALL HIS HOUSEHOLD, ACCORDING TO THE FEELINGS OF HIS HEART AND THE SPIRIT OF THE LORD WHICH WAS IN HIM, HE WAXED OLD.
AND IT CAME TO PASS THAT HE DIED, AND WAS BURIED.
AND IT CAME TO PASS THAT NOT MANY DAYS AFTER HIS DEATH, LAMAN AND LEMUEL AND THE SONS OF ISHMAEL WERE ANGRY WITH ME BECAUSE OF THE ADMONITIONS OF THE LORD.
FOR I, NEPHI, WAS CONSTRAINED TO SPEAK TO THEM, ACCORDING TO HIS WORD; FOR I HAD SPOKEN MANY THINGS TO THEM AS HAD MY FATHER, BEFORE HIS DEATH...
...MANY OF WHICH SAYINGS ARE WRITTEN UPON MY OTHER PLATES.
AND UPON THESE PLATES I WRITE THE THINGS OF MY SOUL, AND MANY OF THE SCRIPTURES WHICH ARE ENGRAVEN UPON THE PLATES OF BRASS.

THE PSALM OF NEPH

FOR MY SOUL DELIGHTETH IN THE SCRIPTURES, AND MY HEART PONDERETH THEM, AND WRITETH THEM FOR THE LEARNING AND THE PROFIT OF MY CHILDREN.

BEHOLD, MY SOUL DELIGHTETH IN THE THINGS OF THE LORD; AND MY HEART PONDERETH CONTINUALLY UPON THE THINGS WHICH I HAVE SEEN AND HEARD.

NEVERTHELESS, NOTWITHSTANDING THE GREAT GOODNESS OF THE LORD, IN SHOWING ME HIS GREAT AND MARVELOUS WORKS, MY HEART EXCLAIMETH: O WRETCHED MAN THAT I AM! YEA, MY HEART SORROWETH BECAUSE OF MY FLESH; MY SOUL GRIEVETH BECAUSE OF MINE INIQUITIES.

I AM ENCOMPASSED ABOUT, BECAUSE OF THE TEMPTATIONS AND THE SINS WHICH DO SO EASILY BESET ME.

AND WHEN I DESIRE TO REJOICE, MY HEART GROANETH BECAUSE OF MY SINS; NEVERTHELESS, I KNOW IN WHOM I HAVE TRUSTED.

MY GOD HATH BEEN MY SUPPORT; HE HATH LED ME THROUGH MINE AFFLICTIONS IN THE WILDERNESS; AND HE HATH PRESERVED ME UPON THE WATERS OF THE GREAT DEEP.

HE HATH FILLED ME WITH HIS LOVE, EVEN UNTO THE CONSUMING OF MY FLESH.

HE HATH CONFOUNDED MINE ENEMIES, UNTO THE CAUSING OF THEM TO QUAKE BEFORE ME.

BEHOLD, HE HATH HEARD MY CRY BY DAY, AND HE HATH GIVEN ME KNOWLEDGE BY VISIONS IN THE NIGHT-TIME.

AND BY DAY HAVE I WAXED BOLD IN MIGHTY PRAYER BEFORE HIM; YEA, MY VOICE HAVE I SENT UP ON HIGH; AND ANGELS CAME DOWN AND MINISTERED UNTO ME.

AND UPON THE WINGS OF HIS SPIRIT HATH MY BODY BEEN CARRIED AWAY UPON EXCEEDINGLY HIGH MOUNTAINS. AND MINE EYES HAVE BEHELD GREAT THINGS, YEA, EVEN TOO GREAT FOR MAN; THEREFORE I WAS BIDDEN THAT I SHOULD NOT WRITE THEM.

O THEN, IF I HAVE SEEN SO GREAT THINGS, IF THE LORD IN HIS CONDESCENSION UNTO THE CHILDREN OF MEN HATH VISITED MEN IN SO MUCH MERCY, WHY SHOULD MY HEART WEEP AND MY SOUL LINGER IN THE VALLEY OF SORROW, AND MY FLESH WASTE AWAY, AND MY STRENGTH SLACKEN, BECAUSE OF MINE AFFLICTIONS?

AND WHY SHOULD I YIELD TO SIN, BECAUSE OF MY FLESH? WHY SHOULD I GIVE WAY TO TEMPTATIONS, THAT THE EVIL ONE HAVE PLACE IN MY HEART TO DESTROY MY PEACE AND AFFLICT MY SOUL? WHY AM I ANGRY BECAUSE OF MINE ENEMY?

AWAKE, MY SOUL! NO LONGER DROOP IN SIN. REJOICE, O MY HEART,
AND GIVE PLACE NO MORE FOR THE ENEMY OF SOUL.

DO NOT ANGER AGAIN BECAUSE OF MINE ENEMIES. DO NOT SLACKEN MY STRENGTH BECAUSE OF MINE AFFLICTIONS.

REJOICE, O MY HEART, AND CRY UNTO THE LORD, AND SAY: O LORD, I WILL PRAISE THEE FOREVER; YEA, MY SOUL WILL REJOICE IN THEE, MY GOD, AND THE ROCK OF MY SALVATION.

O LORD, WILT THOU REDEEM MY SOUL? WILT THOU DELIVER ME OUT OF THE HANDS OF MINE ENEMIES? WILT THOU MAKE ME THAT I MAY SHAKE AT THE APPEARANCE OF SIN?

MAY THE GATES OF HELL BE SHUT CONTINUALLY BEFORE ME, BECAUSE THAT MY HEART IS BROKEN AND MY SPIRIT IS CONTRITE! O LORD, WILT THOU NOT SHUT THE GATES OF THY RIGHTEOUSNESS BEFORE ME, THAT I MAY WALK IN THE PATH OF THE LOW VALLEY, THAT I MAY BE STRICT IN THE PLAIN ROAD!

O LORD, WILT THOU ENCIRCLE ME AROUND IN THE ROBE OF THY RIGHTEOUSNESS! O LORD, WILT THOU MAKE A WAY FOR MINE ESCAPE BEFORE MINE ENEMIES! WILT THOU MAKE MY PATH STRAIGHT BEFORE ME! WILT THOU NOT PLACE A STUMBLING BLOCK IN MY WAY--BUT THAT THOU WOULDST CLEAR MY WAY BEFORE ME, AND HEDGE NOT UP MY WAY, BUT THE WAYS OF MINE ENEMY.

O LORD, I HAVE TRUSTED IN THEE, AND I WILL TRUST IN THEE FOREVER. I WILL NOT PUT MY TRUST IN THE ARM OF FLESH; FOR I KNOW THAT CURSED IS HE THAT PUTTETH HIS TRUST IN THE ARM OF FLESH. YEA, CURSED IS HE THAT PUTTETH HIS TRUST IN MAN OR MAKETH FLESH HIS ARM.

YEA, I KNOW THAT GOD WILL GIVE LIBERALLY TO HIM THAT ASKETH.

YEA, MY GOD WILL GIVE ME, IF I ASK NOT AMISS; THEREFORE I WILL LIFT UP MY VOICE UNTO THEE; YEA, I WILL CRY UNTO THEE, MY GOD, THE ROCK OF MY RIGHTEOUSNESS.

BEHOLD, MY VOICE SHALL FOREVER ASCEND UP UNTO THEE, MY ROCK AND MINE EVERLASTING GOD. AMEN.

CHAPTER 5
IT CAME TO PASS THAT I, NEPHI, DID CRY MUCH UNTO THE LORD MY GOD, BECAUSE OF THE ANGER OF MY BRETHREN.
AND THEIR ANGER DID INCREASE AGAINST ME SO MUCH THAT THEY DID CONSPIRE AND COMMIT TO TAKE AWAY MY LIFE.
OUR YOUNGER BROTHER, NEPHI THINKS TO RULE OVER US.
WE HAVE HAD TOO MUCH TRIAL BECAUSE OF HIM.
BEHOLD, WE WILL NOT HAVE HIM TO BE OUR RULER. LEHI IS DEAD AND SO IT IS FOR US, WHO ARE THE ELDER BRETHREN, TO RULE OVER THIS PEOPLE.
LET US BE DONE WITH HIM SOON AND FINALLY.
CAN WE NOW SLAY HIM, THAT WE MAY BE FREE FROM HIS HUMILIATIONS?

AND IT CAME TO PASS THAT THE LORD DID WARN ME, THAT I, NEPHI, SHOULD DEPART FROM LAMAN AND LEMUEL AND FLEE INTO THE WILDERNESS, AND ALL THOSE WHO WOULD GO WITH ME.

AND SO I TOOK MY FAMILY, AND ALSO ZORAM AND HIS FAMILY, AND SAM, MY ELDER BROTHER AND HIS FAMILY, AND JACOB AND JOSEPH, MY YOUNGER BRETHREN, AND ALSO MY SISTERS, AND ALL THOSE WHO WOULD GO WITH ME.
AND ALL THOSE WHO WOULD GO WITH ME WERE THOSE WHO BELIEVED IN THE WARNINGS AND THE REVELATIONS OF GOD; WHEREFORE, THEY DID HEARKEN UNTO MY WORDS.

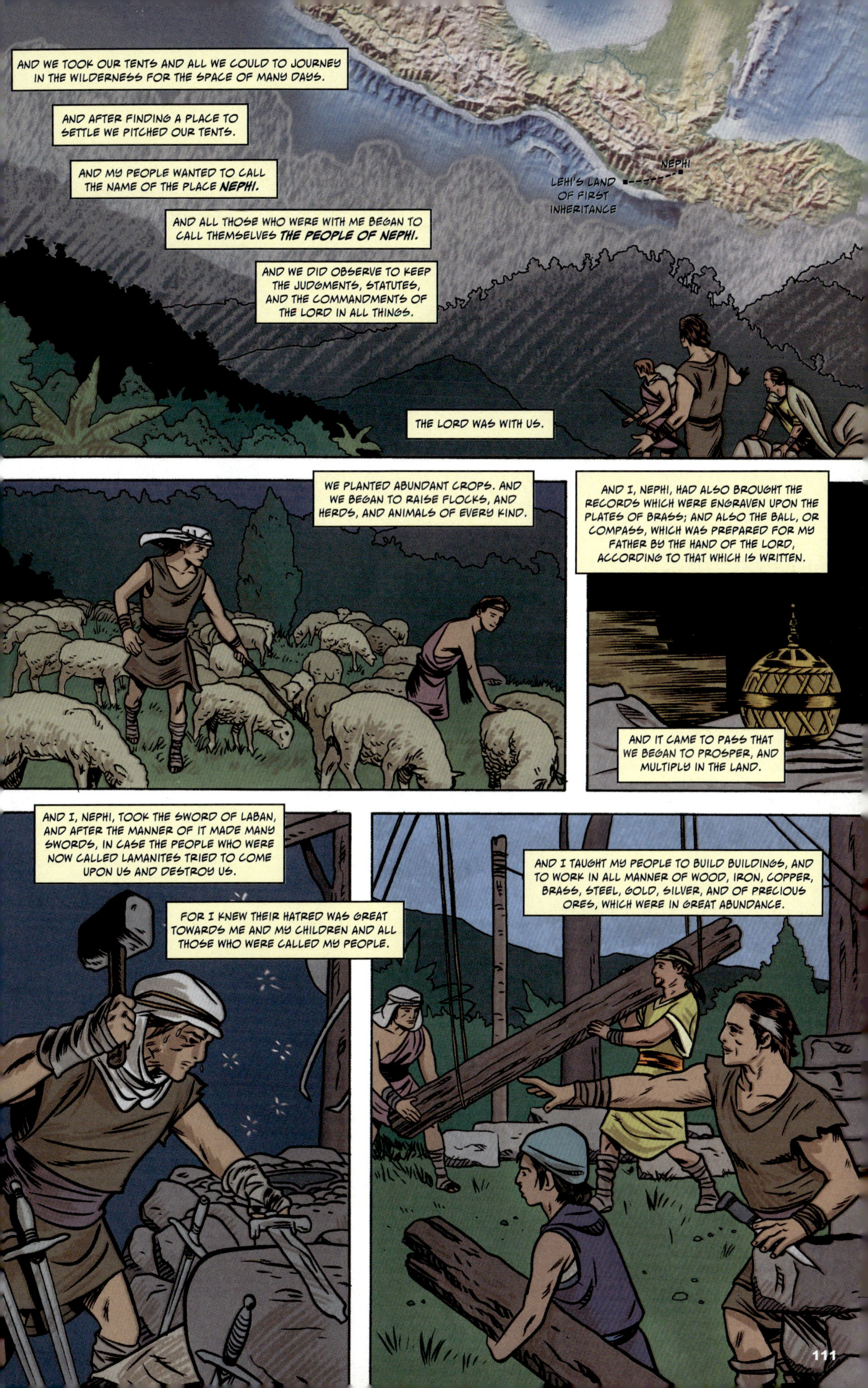
AND WE TOOK OUR TENTS AND ALL WE COULD TO JOURNEY IN THE WILDERNESS FOR THE SPACE OF MANY DAYS.
AND AFTER FINDING A PLACE TO SETTLE WE PITCHED OUR TENTS.
AND MY PEOPLE WANTED TO CALL THE NAME OF THE PLACE NEPHI.
AND ALL THOSE WHO WERE WITH ME BEGAN TO CALL THEMSELVES THE PEOPLE OF NEPHI.
AND WE DID OBSERVE TO KEEP THE JUDGMENTS, STATUTES, AND THE COMMANDMENTS OF THE LORD IN ALL THINGS.
NEPHI
LEHI'S LAND OF FIRST INHERITANCE
THE LORD WAS WITH US.
WE PLANTED ABUNDANT CROPS. AND WE BEGAN TO RAISE FLOCKS, AND HERDS, AND ANIMALS OF EVERY KIND.
AND I, NEPHI, HAD ALSO BROUGHT THE RECORDS WHICH WERE ENGRAVEN UPON THE PLATES OF BRASS; AND ALSO THE BALL, OR COMPASS, WHICH WAS PREPARED FOR MY FATHER BY THE HAND OF THE LORD, ACCORDING TO THAT WHICH IS WRITTEN.
AND IT CAME TO PASS THAT WE BEGAN TO PROSPER, AND MULTIPLY IN THE LAND.
AND I, NEPHI, TOOK THE SWORD OF LABAN, AND AFTER THE MANNER OF IT MADE MANY SWORDS, IN CASE THE PEOPLE WHO WERE NOW CALLED LAMANITES TRIED TO COME UPON US AND DESTROY US.
FOR I KNEW THEIR HATRED WAS GREAT TOWARDS ME AND MY CHILDREN AND ALL THOSE WHO WERE CALLED MY PEOPLE.
AND I TAUGHT MY PEOPLE TO BUILD BUILDINGS, AND TO WORK IN ALL MANNER OF WOOD, IRON, COPPER, BRASS, STEEL, GOLD, SILVER, AND OF PRECIOUS ORES, WHICH WERE IN GREAT ABUNDANCE.

AND I, NEPHI, DID BUILD A TEMPLE.
I CONSTRUCTED IT AFTER THE MANNER OF THE TEMPLE OF SOLOMON...
...EXCEPT IT WAS NOT BUILT OF SO MANY PRECIOUS THINGS SINCE THEY WERE NOT TO BE FOUND UPON THE LAND.
AND SO, IT COULD NOT BE BUILT EXACTLY LIKE SOLOMON'S TEMPLE.
BUT THE WORKMANSHIP OF IT WAS EXCEEDINGLY FINE BECAUSE I HAD TAUGHT MY PEOPLE TO BE INDUSTRIOUS, AND TO LABOR WITH THEIR HANDS.

AND IT CAME TO PASS THAT THEY WANTED ME TO BE THEIR KING.
BUT I, NEPHI, WAS DESIROUS THAT THEY SHOULD HAVE NO KING; NEVERTHELESS, I DID EVERYTHING I COULD FOR THEM WITHIN MY POWER.
AND BEHOLD, THE WORDS OF THE LORD HAD BEEN FULFILLED UNTO MY BRETHREN, WHICH HE SPAKE CONCERNING THEM, THAT I SHOULD BE THEIR RULER AND THEIR TEACHER.
WHEREFORE, I HAD BEEN THEIR RULER AND THEIR TEACHER, ACCORDING TO THE COMMANDMENTS OF THE LORD, UNTIL THE TIME THEY SOUGHT TO TAKE AWAY MY LIFE.
WHEREFORE, THE WORD OF THE LORD WAS FULFILLED WHICH HE SPAKE UNTO ME, SAYING THAT: INASMUCH AS THEY WILL NOT HEARKEN UNTO THY WORDS THEY SHALL BE CUT OFF FROM THE PRESENCE OF THE LORD. AND BEHOLD, THEY WERE CUT OFF FROM HIS PRESENCE.

AND HE HAD CAUSED THE CURSING TO COME UPON THEM, EVEN A SORE CURSING, BECAUSE OF THEIR INIQUITY.
FOR BEHOLD, THEY HAD HARDENED THEIR HEARTS AGAINST HIM, THAT THEY HAD BECOME LIKE UNTO A FLINT; WHEREFORE, AS THEY WERE WHITE, AND EXCEEDINGLY FAIR AND DELIGHTSOME, THAT THEY MIGHT NOT BE ENTICING UNTO MY PEOPLE THE LORD GOD DID CAUSE A SKIN OF BLACKNESS TO COME UPON THEM.
AND THUS SAITH THE LORD GOD: I WILL CAUSE THAT THEY SHALL BE LOATHSOME UNTO THY PEOPLE, SAVE THEY SHALL REPENT OF THEIR INIQUITIES.
AND CURSED SHALL BE THE SEED OF HIM THAT MIXETH WITH THEIR SEED; FOR THEY SHALL BE CURSED EVEN WITH THE SAME CURSING. AND THE LORD SPAKE IT, AND IT WAS DONE.
AND BECAUSE OF THEIR CURSING WHICH WAS UPON THEM THEY DID BECOME AN IDLE PEOPLE, FULL OF MISCHIEF AND SUBTLETY, AND DID SEEK IN THE WILDERNESS FOR BEASTS OF PREY.
AND THE LORD GOD SAID UNTO ME: THEY SHALL BE A SCOURGE UNTO THY SEED, TO STIR THEM UP IN REMEMBRANCE OF ME; AND INASMUCH AS THEY WILL NOT REMEMBER ME, AND HEARKEN UNTO MY WORDS, THEY SHALL SCOURGE THEM EVEN UNTO DESTRUCTION.

AND IT CAME TO PASS THAT I, NEPHI, DID CONSECRATE JACOB AND JOSEPH, THAT THEY SHOULD BE PRIESTS AND TEACHERS OVER THE LAND OF MY PEOPLE.
AND IT CAME TO PASS THAT WE LIVED AFTER THE MANNER OF HAPPINESS.
AND I, NEPHI, HAD KEPT THE RECORDS UPON MY PLATES, WHICH I HAD MADE, OF MY PEOPLE THUS FAR.
AND IT CAME TO PASS THAT THE LORD GOD SAID UNTO ME: MAKE OTHER PLATES; AND THOU SHALT ENGRAVEN MANY THINGS UPON THEM WHICH ARE GOOD IN MY SIGHT, FOR THE PROFIT OF THY PEOPLE.
WHEREFORE, I, NEPHI, TO BE OBEDIENT TO THE COMMANDMENTS OF THE LORD, WENT AND MADE THESE PLATES UPON WHICH I HAVE ENGRAVEN THESE THINGS.
AND I ENGRAVED THAT WHICH IS PLEASING UNTO GOD. AND IF MY PEOPLE ARE PLEASED WITH THE THINGS OF GOD THEY WILL BE PLEASED WITH MINE ENGRAVINGS WHICH ARE UPON THESE PLATES.
AND IF MY PEOPLE DESIRE TO KNOW THE MORE PARTICULAR PART OF THE HISTORY OF MY PEOPLE THEY MUST SEARCH MY OTHER PLATES.
AND IT SUFFICETH ME TO SAY THAT ***FORTY YEARS*** HAD PASSED AWAY, AND WE HAD ALREADY HAD WARS AND CONTENTIONS WITH OUR BRETHREN.

CHAPTER 6
BETWEEN 559 AND 545 B.C.
THE WORDS OF JACOB, THE BROTHER OF NEPHI, WHICH HE SPAKE UNTO THE PEOPLE OF NEPHI:
BEHOLD, MY BELOVED BRETHREN, I, JACOB, HAVING BEEN CALLED OF GOD, AND ORDAINED AFTER THE MANNER OF HIS HOLY ORDER, AND HAVING BEEN CONSECRATED BY MY BROTHER NEPHI, UNTO WHOM YOU LOOK AS A KING OR A PROTECTOR, AND ON WHOM YOU DEPEND FOR SAFETY, BEHOLD YOU KNOW THAT I HAVE SPOKEN UNTO YOU EXCEEDINGLY MANY THINGS.
AND NOW I WOULD SPEAK UNTO YOU CONCERNING THINGS WHICH ARE, AND WHICH ARE TO COME; WHEREFORE, I WILL READ YOU THE WORDS OF ISAIAH. AND THEY ARE THE WORDS WHICH MY BROTHER HAS DESIRED THAT I SHOULD SPEAK UNTO YOU. AND I SPEAK UNTO YOU FOR YOUR SAKES, THAT YE MAY LEARN AND GLORIFY THE NAME OF YOUR GOD.
THE WORDS WHICH I SHALL READ ARE THEY WHICH ISAIAH SPAKE CONCERNING ALL THE HOUSE OF ISRAEL; WHEREFORE, THEY MAY BE LIKENED UNTO YOU, FOR YOU ARE OF THE HOUSE OF ISRAEL.
AND NOW, THESE ARE THE WORDS:
"THUS SAITH THE LORD GOD: BEHOLD, I WILL LIFT UP MINE HAND TO THE GENTILES, AND SET UP MY STANDARD TO THE PEOPLE; AND THEY SHALL BRING THY SONS IN THEIR ARMS, AND THY DAUGHTERS SHALL BE CARRIED UPON THEIR SHOULDERS.
AND KINGS SHALL BE THY NURSING FATHERS, AND THEIR QUEENS THY NURSING MOTHERS; THEY SHALL BOW DOWN TO THEE WITH THEIR FACES TOWARDS THE EARTH, AND LICK UP THE DUST OF THY FEET; AND THOU SHALT KNOW THAT I AM THE LORD; FOR THEY SHALL NOT BE ASHAMED THAT WAIT FOR ME."
AND NOW I, JACOB, WOULD SPEAK SOMEWHAT CONCERNING THESE WORDS.
FOR BEHOLD, THE LORD HAS SHOWN ME THAT THOSE WHO WERE AT JERUSALEM, FROM WHENCE WE CAME, HAVE BEEN SLAIN AND CARRIED AWAY CAPTIVE.
NEVERTHELESS, THE LORD HAS SHOWN UNTO ME THAT THEY SHOULD RETURN AGAIN. AND HE ALSO HAS SHOWN UNTO ME THAT THE LORD GOD, THE HOLY ONE OF ISRAEL, SHOULD MANIFEST HIMSELF UNTO THEM IN THE FLESH; AND AFTER HE SHOULD MANIFEST HIMSELF THEY SHOULD SCOURGE HIM AND CRUCIFY HIM, ACCORDING TO THE WORDS OF THE ANGEL WHO SPAKE IT UNTO ME.
AND AFTER THEY HAVE HARDENED THEIR HEARTS AND STIFFENED THEIR NECKS AGAINST THE HOLY ONE OF ISRAEL, BEHOLD, THE JUDGMENTS OF THE HOLY ONE OF ISRAEL SHALL COME UPON THEM. AND THE DAY COMETH THAT THEY SHALL BE SMITTEN AND AFFLICTED.
WHEREFORE, AFTER THEY ARE DRIVEN TO AND FRO, FOR THUS SAITH THE ANGEL, MANY SHALL BE AFFLICTED IN THE FLESH, AND SHALL NOT BE SUFFERED TO PERISH, BECAUSE OF THE PRAYERS OF THE FAITHFUL; THEY SHALL BE SCATTERED, AND SMITTEN, AND HATED; NEVERTHELESS, THE LORD WILL BE MERCIFUL UNTO THEM, THAT WHEN THEY SHALL COME TO THE KNOWLEDGE OF THEIR REDEEMER, THEY SHALL BE GATHERED TOGETHER AGAIN TO THE LANDS OF THEIR INHERITANCE.
AND BLESSED ARE THE GENTILES, THEY OF WHOM THE PROPHET HAS WRITTEN; FOR BEHOLD, IF IT SO BE THAT THEY SHALL REPENT AND FIGHT NOT AGAINST ZION, AND DO NOT UNITE THEMSELVES TO THAT GREAT AND ABOMINABLE CHURCH, THEY SHALL BE SAVED; FOR THE LORD GOD WILL FULFIL HIS COVENANTS WHICH HE HAS MADE UNTO HIS CHILDREN; AND FOR THIS CAUSE THE PROPHET HAS WRITTEN THESE THINGS.

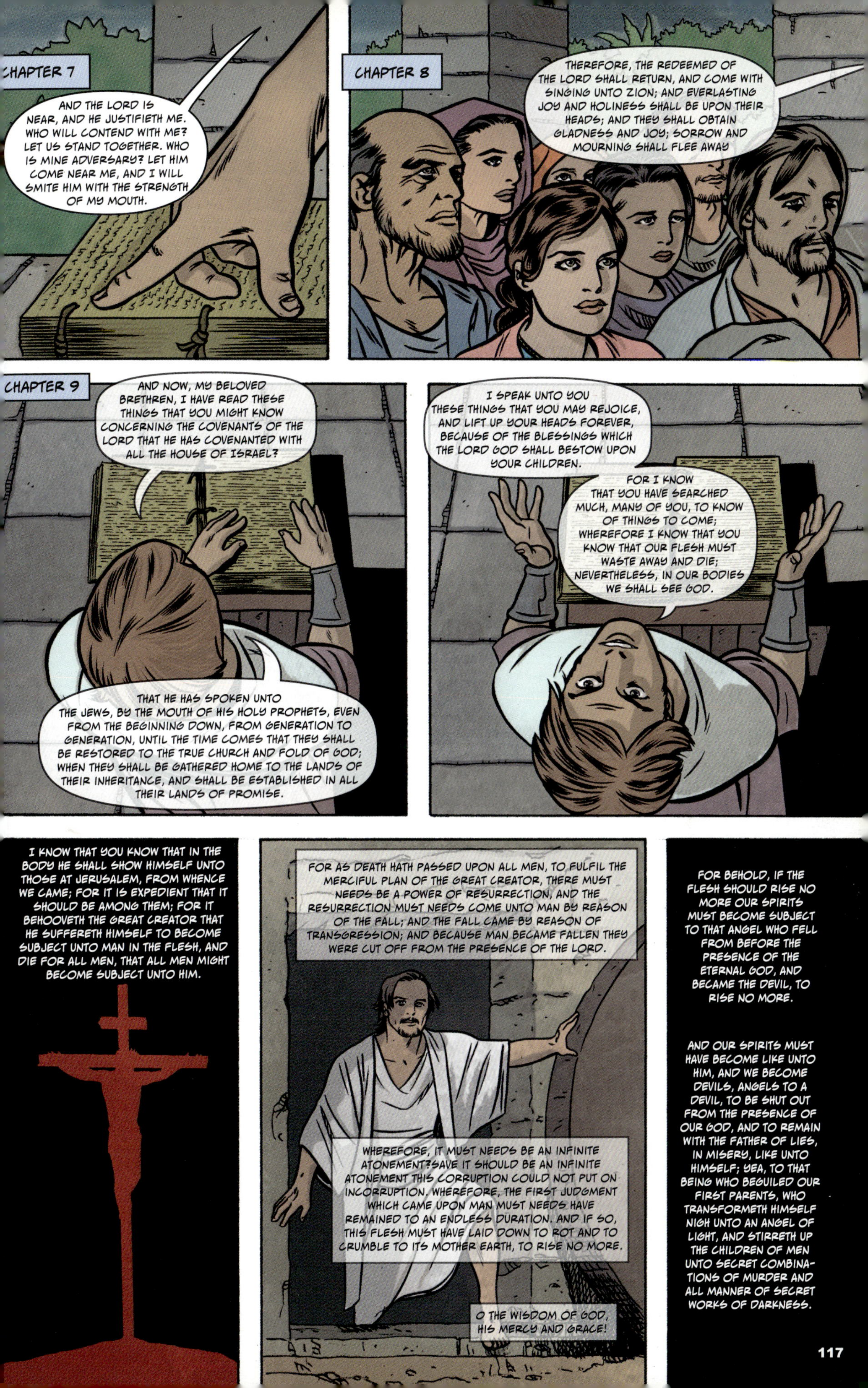
CHAPTER 7
AND THE LORD IS NEAR, AND HE JUSTIFIETH ME. WHO WILL CONTEND WITH ME? LET US STAND TOGETHER. WHO IS MINE ADVERSARY? LET HIM COME NEAR ME, AND I WILL SMITE HIM WITH THE STRENGTH OF MY MOUTH.
CHAPTER 8
THEREFORE, THE REDEEMED OF THE LORD SHALL RETURN, AND COME WITH SINGING UNTO ZION; AND EVERLASTING JOY AND HOLINESS SHALL BE UPON THEIR HEADS; AND THEY SHALL OBTAIN GLADNESS AND JOY; SORROW AND MOURNING SHALL FLEE AWAY
CHAPTER 9
AND NOW, MY BELOVED BRETHREN, I HAVE READ THESE THINGS THAT YOU MIGHT KNOW CONCERNING THE COVENANTS OF THE LORD THAT HE HAS COVENANTED WITH ALL THE HOUSE OF ISRAEL?
THAT HE HAS SPOKEN UNTO THE JEWS, BY THE MOUTH OF HIS HOLY PROPHETS, EVEN FROM THE BEGINNING DOWN, FROM GENERATION TO GENERATION, UNTIL THE TIME COMES THAT THEY SHALL BE RESTORED TO THE TRUE CHURCH AND FOLD OF GOD; WHEN THEY SHALL BE GATHERED HOME TO THE LANDS OF THEIR INHERITANCE, AND SHALL BE ESTABLISHED IN ALL THEIR LANDS OF PROMISE.
I SPEAK UNTO YOU THESE THINGS THAT YOU MAY REJOICE, AND LIFT UP YOUR HEADS FOREVER, BECAUSE OF THE BLESSINGS WHICH THE LORD GOD SHALL BESTOW UPON YOUR CHILDREN.
FOR I KNOW THAT YOU HAVE SEARCHED MUCH, MANY OF YOU, TO KNOW OF THINGS TO COME; WHEREFORE I KNOW THAT YOU KNOW THAT OUR FLESH MUST WASTE AWAY AND DIE; NEVERTHELESS, IN OUR BODIES WE SHALL SEE GOD.
I KNOW THAT YOU KNOW THAT IN THE BODY HE SHALL SHOW HIMSELF UNTO THOSE AT JERUSALEM, FROM WHENCE WE CAME; FOR IT IS EXPEDIENT THAT IT SHOULD BE AMONG THEM; FOR IT BEHOOVETH THE GREAT CREATOR THAT HE SUFFERETH HIMSELF TO BECOME SUBJECT UNTO MAN IN THE FLESH, AND DIE FOR ALL MEN, THAT ALL MEN MIGHT BECOME SUBJECT UNTO HIM.
FOR AS DEATH HATH PASSED UPON ALL MEN, TO FULFIL THE MERCIFUL PLAN OF THE GREAT CREATOR, THERE MUST NEEDS BE A POWER OF RESURRECTION, AND THE RESURRECTION MUST NEEDS COME UNTO MAN BY REASON OF THE FALL; AND THE FALL CAME BY REASON OF TRANSGRESSION; AND BECAUSE MAN BECAME FALLEN THEY WERE CUT OFF FROM THE PRESENCE OF THE LORD.
WHEREFORE, IT MUST NEEDS BE AN INFINITE ATONEMENT?SAVE IT SHOULD BE AN INFINITE ATONEMENT THIS CORRUPTION COULD NOT PUT ON INCORRUPTION. WHEREFORE, THE FIRST JUDGMENT WHICH CAME UPON MAN MUST NEEDS HAVE REMAINED TO AN ENDLESS DURATION. AND IF SO, THIS FLESH MUST HAVE LAID DOWN TO ROT AND TO CRUMBLE TO ITS MOTHER EARTH, TO RISE NO MORE.
O THE WISDOM OF GOD, HIS MERCY AND GRACE!
FOR BEHOLD, IF THE FLESH SHOULD RISE NO MORE OUR SPIRITS MUST BECOME SUBJECT TO THAT ANGEL WHO FELL FROM BEFORE THE PRESENCE OF THE ETERNAL GOD, AND BECAME THE DEVIL, TO RISE NO MORE.
AND OUR SPIRITS MUST HAVE BECOME LIKE UNTO HIM, AND WE BECOME DEVILS, ANGELS TO A DEVIL, TO BE SHUT OUT FROM THE PRESENCE OF OUR GOD, AND TO REMAIN WITH THE FATHER OF LIES, IN MISERY, LIKE UNTO HIMSELF; YEA, TO THAT BEING WHO BEGUILED OUR FIRST PARENTS, WHO TRANSFORMETH HIMSELF NIGH UNTO AN ANGEL OF LIGHT, AND STIRRETH UP THE CHILDREN OF MEN UNTO SECRET COMBINATIONS OF MURDER AND ALL MANNER OF SECRET WORKS OF DARKNESS.

O HOW GREAT THE GOODNESS OF OUR GOD, WHO PREPARES A WAY FOR OUR ESCAPE FROM THE GRASP OF THIS AWFUL MONSTER; YEA, THAT MONSTER, DEATH AND HELL, WHICH I CALL THE DEATH OF THE BODY, AND ALSO THE DEATH OF THE SPIRIT.
AND BECAUSE OF THE WAY OF DELIVERANCE OF OUR GOD, THE HOLY ONE OF ISRAEL, THIS DEATH, OF WHICH I HAVE SPOKEN, WHICH IS THE TEMPORAL, SHALL DELIVER UP ITS DEAD; WHICH DEATH IS THE GRAVE.
AND THIS DEATH OF WHICH I HAVE SPOKEN, WHICH IS THE SPIRITUAL DEATH, SHALL DELIVER UP ITS DEAD; WHICH SPIRITUAL DEATH IS HELL; WHEREFORE, DEATH AND HELL MUST DELIVER UP THEIR DEAD, AND HELL MUST DELIVER UP ITS CAPTIVE SPIRITS, AND THE GRAVE MUST DELIVER UP ITS CAPTIVE BODIES, AND THE BODIES AND THE SPIRITS OF MEN WILL BE RESTORED ONE TO THE OTHER; AND IT IS BY THE POWER OF THE RESURRECTION OF THE HOLY ONE OF ISRAEL.
O HOW GREAT THE PLAN OF OUR GOD! FOR ON THE OTHER HAND, THE PARADISE OF GOD MUST DELIVER UP THE SPIRITS OF THE RIGHTEOUS, AND THE GRAVE DELIVER UP THE BODY OF THE RIGHTEOUS; AND THE SPIRIT AND THE BODY IS RESTORED TO ITSELF AGAIN, AND ALL MEN BECOME INCORRUPTIBLE, AND IMMORTAL, AND THEY ARE LIVING SOULS, HAVING A PERFECT KNOWLEDGE LIKE UNTO US IN THE FLESH, SAVE IT BE THAT OUR KNOWLEDGE SHALL BE PERFECT.
WHEREFORE, WE SHALL HAVE A PERFECT KNOWLEDGE OF ALL OUR GUILT, AND OUR UNCLEANNESS, AND OUR NAKEDNESS; AND THE RIGHTEOUS SHALL HAVE A PERFECT KNOWLEDGE OF THEIR ENJOYMENT, AND THEIR RIGHTEOUSNESS, BEING CLOTHED WITH PURITY, YEA, EVEN WITH THE ROBE OF RIGHTEOUSNESS.
AND IT SHALL COME TO PASS THAT WHEN ALL MEN SHALL HAVE PASSED FROM THIS FIRST DEATH UNTO LIFE, INSOMUCH AS THEY HAVE BECOME IMMORTAL, THEY MUST APPEAR BEFORE THE JUDGMENT-SEAT OF THE HOLY ONE OF ISRAEL; AND THEN COMETH THE JUDGMENT, AND THEN MUST THEY BE JUDGED ACCORDING TO THE HOLY JUDGMENT OF GOD.
AND ASSUREDLY, AS THE LORD LIVES, FOR THE LORD GOD HAS SPOKEN IT, AND IT IS HIS ETERNAL WORD, WHICH CANNOT PASS AWAY, THAT THEY WHO ARE RIGHTEOUS SHALL BE RIGHTEOUS STILL...
...AND THEY WHO ARE FILTHY SHALL BE FILTHY STILL; WHEREFORE, THEY WHO ARE FILTHY ARE THE DEVIL AND HIS ANGELS; AND THEY SHALL GO AWAY INTO EVERLASTING FIRE, PREPARED FOR THEM; AND THEIR TORMENT IS AS A LAKE OF FIRE AND BRIMSTONE, WHOSE FLAME ASCENDS UP FOREVER AND EVER AND HAS NO END.
O THE GREATNESS AND THE JUSTICE OF OUR GOD! FOR HE EXECUTES ALL HIS WORDS, AND THEY HAVE GONE FORTH OUT OF HIS MOUTH, AND HIS LAW MUST BE FULFILLED.
BUT, BEHOLD, THE RIGHTEOUS, THE SAINTS OF THE HOLY ONE OF ISRAEL, THEY WHO HAVE BELIEVED IN THE HOLY ONE OF ISRAEL, THEY WHO HAVE ENDURED THE CROSSES OF THE WORLD, AND DESPISED THE SHAME OF IT, THEY SHALL INHERIT THE KINGDOM OF GOD, WHICH WAS PREPARED FOR THEM FROM THE FOUNDATION OF THE WORLD, AND THEIR JOY SHALL BE FULL FOREVER.
AND HE COMES INTO THE WORLD THAT HE MAY SAVE ALL MEN IF THEY WILL HEARKEN UNTO HIS VOICE; FOR BEHOLD, HE SUFFERS THE PAINS OF ALL MEN, THE PAINS OF EVERY LIVING CREATURE, BOTH MEN, WOMEN, AND CHILDREN, WHO BELONG TO THE FAMILY OF ADAM.
AND HE SUFFERS THIS THAT THE RESURRECTION MIGHT PASS UPON ALL MEN, THAT ALL MIGHT STAND BEFORE HIM AT THE GREAT AND JUDGMENT DAY.

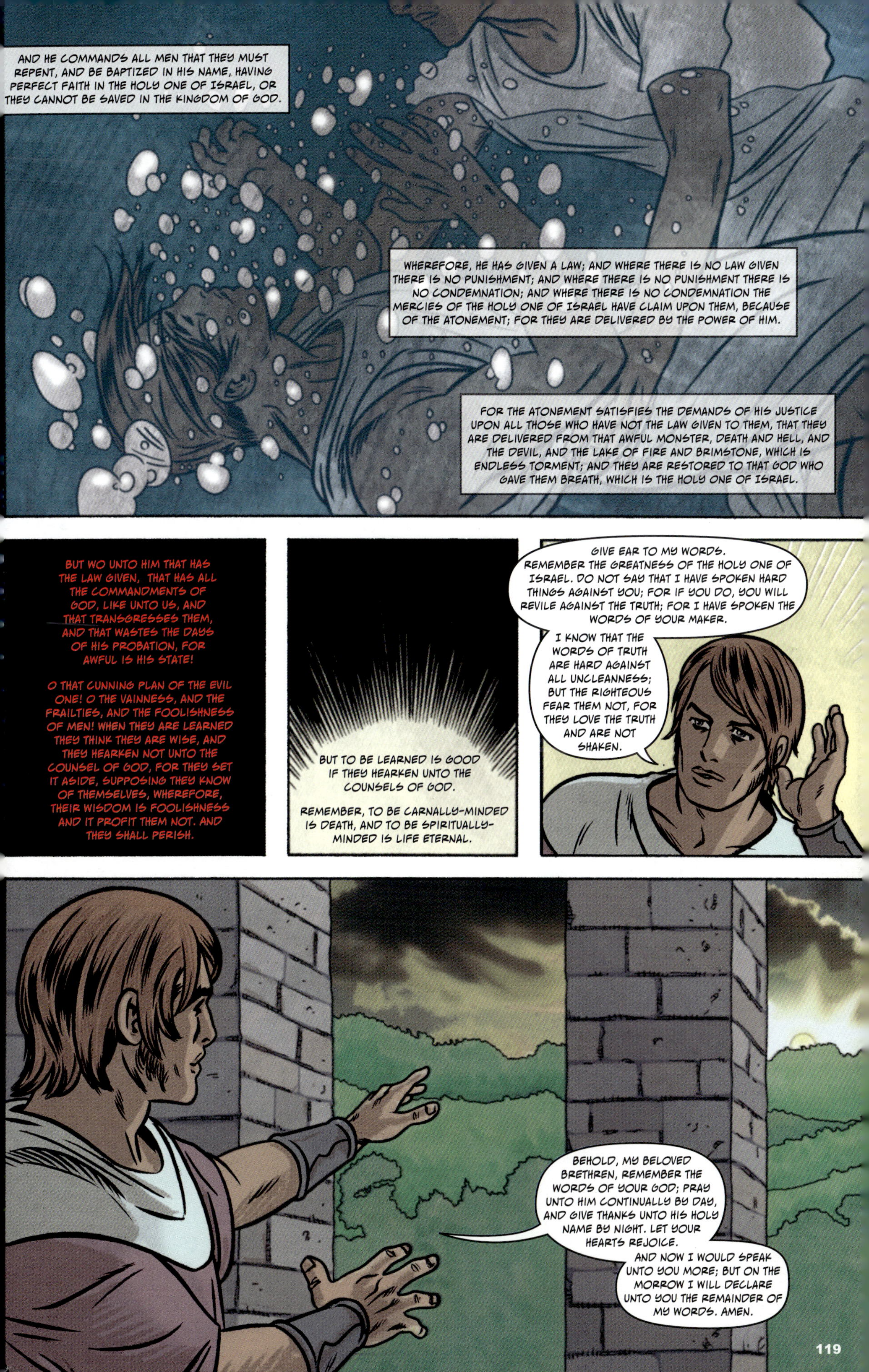
AND HE COMMANDS ALL MEN THAT THEY MUST REPENT, AND BE BAPTIZED IN HIS NAME, HAVING PERFECT FAITH IN THE HOLY ONE OF ISRAEL, OR THEY CANNOT BE SAVED IN THE KINGDOM OF GOD.
WHEREFORE, HE HAS GIVEN A LAW; AND WHERE THERE IS NO LAW GIVEN THERE IS NO PUNISHMENT; AND WHERE THERE IS NO PUNISHMENT THERE IS NO CONDEMNATION; AND WHERE THERE IS NO CONDEMNATION THE MERCIES OF THE HOLY ONE OF ISRAEL HAVE CLAIM UPON THEM, BECAUSE OF THE ATONEMENT; FOR THEY ARE DELIVERED BY THE POWER OF HIM.
FOR THE ATONEMENT SATISFIES THE DEMANDS OF HIS JUSTICE UPON ALL THOSE WHO HAVE NOT THE LAW GIVEN TO THEM, THAT THEY ARE DELIVERED FROM THAT AWFUL MONSTER, DEATH AND HELL, AND THE DEVIL, AND THE LAKE OF FIRE AND BRIMSTONE, WHICH IS ENDLESS TORMENT; AND THEY ARE RESTORED TO THAT GOD WHO GAVE THEM BREATH, WHICH IS THE HOLY ONE OF ISRAEL.
BUT WO UNTO HIM THAT HAS THE LAW GIVEN, THAT HAS ALL THE COMMANDMENTS OF GOD, LIKE UNTO US, AND THAT TRANSGRESSES THEM, AND THAT WASTES THE DAYS OF HIS PROBATION, FOR AWFUL IS HIS STATE!
O THAT CUNNING PLAN OF THE EVIL ONE! O THE VAINNESS, AND THE FRAILTIES, AND THE FOOLISHNESS OF MEN! WHEN THEY ARE LEARNED THEY THINK THEY ARE WISE, AND THEY HEARKEN NOT UNTO THE COUNSEL OF GOD, FOR THEY SET IT ASIDE, SUPPOSING THEY KNOW OF THEMSELVES, WHEREFORE, THEIR WISDOM IS FOOLISHNESS AND IT PROFIT THEM NOT. AND THEY SHALL PERISH.
BUT TO BE LEARNED IS GOOD IF THEY HEARKEN UNTO THE COUNSELS OF GOD.
REMEMBER, TO BE CARNALLY-MINDED IS DEATH, AND TO BE SPIRITUALLY-MINDED IS LIFE ETERNAL.
GIVE EAR TO MY WORDS. REMEMBER THE GREATNESS OF THE HOLY ONE OF ISRAEL. DO NOT SAY THAT I HAVE SPOKEN HARD THINGS AGAINST YOU; FOR IF YOU DO, YOU WILL REVILE AGAINST THE TRUTH; FOR I HAVE SPOKEN THE WORDS OF YOUR MAKER.
I KNOW THAT THE WORDS OF TRUTH ARE HARD AGAINST ALL UNCLEANNESS; BUT THE RIGHTEOUS FEAR THEM NOT, FOR THEY LOVE THE TRUTH AND ARE NOT SHAKEN.
BEHOLD, MY BELOVED BRETHREN, REMEMBER THE WORDS OF YOUR GOD; PRAY UNTO HIM CONTINUALLY BY DAY, AND GIVE THANKS UNTO HIS HOLY NAME BY NIGHT. LET YOUR HEARTS REJOICE.
AND NOW I WOULD SPEAK UNTO YOU MORE; BUT ON THE MORROW I WILL DECLARE UNTO YOU THE REMAINDER OF MY WORDS. AMEN.

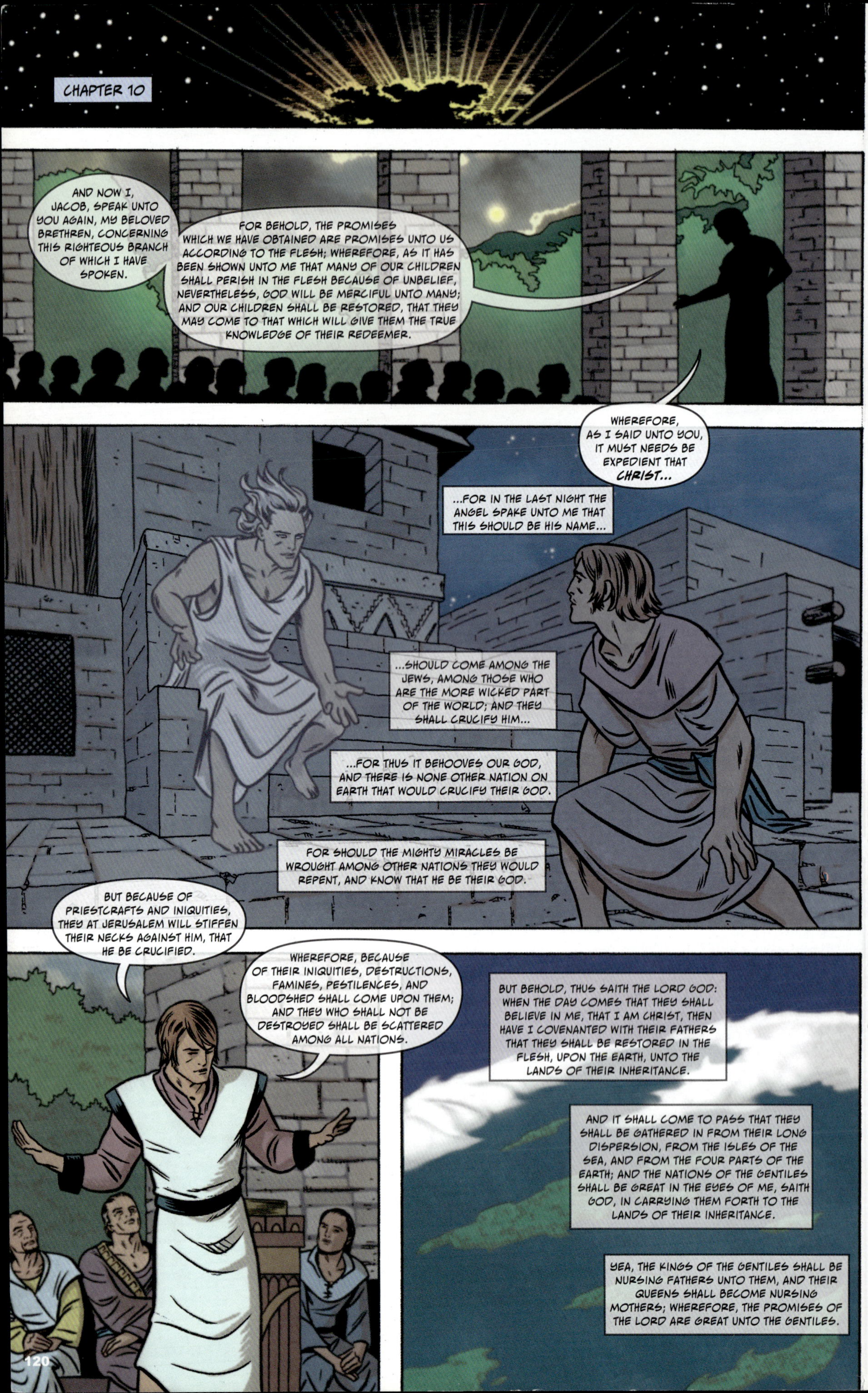
CHAPTER 10
AND NOW I, JACOB, SPEAK UNTO YOU AGAIN, MY BELOVED BRETHREN, CONCERNING THIS RIGHTEOUS BRANCH OF WHICH I HAVE SPOKEN.
FOR BEHOLD, THE PROMISES WHICH WE HAVE OBTAINED ARE PROMISES UNTO US ACCORDING TO THE FLESH; WHEREFORE, AS IT HAS BEEN SHOWN UNTO ME THAT MANY OF OUR CHILDREN SHALL PERISH IN THE FLESH BECAUSE OF UNBELIEF, NEVERTHELESS, GOD WILL BE MERCIFUL UNTO MANY; AND OUR CHILDREN SHALL BE RESTORED, THAT THEY MAY COME TO THAT WHICH WILL GIVE THEM THE TRUE KNOWLEDGE OF THEIR REDEEMER.
WHEREFORE, AS I SAID UNTO YOU, IT MUST NEEDS BE EXPEDIENT THAT CHRIST...
...FOR IN THE LAST NIGHT THE ANGEL SPAKE UNTO ME THAT THIS SHOULD BE HIS NAME...
...SHOULD COME AMONG THE JEWS, AMONG THOSE WHO ARE THE MORE WICKED PART OF THE WORLD; AND THEY SHALL CRUCIFY HIM...
...FOR THUS IT BEHOOVES OUR GOD, AND THERE IS NONE OTHER NATION ON EARTH THAT WOULD CRUCIFY THEIR GOD.
FOR SHOULD THE MIGHTY MIRACLES BE WROUGHT AMONG OTHER NATIONS THEY WOULD REPENT, AND KNOW THAT HE BE THEIR GOD.
BUT BECAUSE OF PRIESTCRAFTS AND INIQUITIES, THEY AT JERUSALEM WILL STIFFEN THEIR NECKS AGAINST HIM, THAT HE BE CRUCIFIED.
WHEREFORE, BECAUSE OF THEIR INIQUITIES, DESTRUCTIONS, FAMINES, PESTILENCES, AND BLOODSHED SHALL COME UPON THEM; AND THEY WHO SHALL NOT BE DESTROYED SHALL BE SCATTERED AMONG ALL NATIONS.
BUT BEHOLD, THUS SAITH THE LORD GOD: WHEN THE DAY COMES THAT THEY SHALL BELIEVE IN ME, THAT I AM CHRIST, THEN HAVE I COVENANTED WITH THEIR FATHERS THAT THEY SHALL BE RESTORED IN THE FLESH, UPON THE EARTH, UNTO THE LANDS OF THEIR INHERITANCE.
AND IT SHALL COME TO PASS THAT THEY SHALL BE GATHERED IN FROM THEIR LONG DISPERSION, FROM THE ISLES OF THE SEA, AND FROM THE FOUR PARTS OF THE EARTH; AND THE NATIONS OF THE GENTILES SHALL BE GREAT IN THE EYES OF ME, SAITH GOD, IN CARRYING THEM FORTH TO THE LANDS OF THEIR INHERITANCE.
YEA, THE KINGS OF THE GENTILES SHALL BE NURSING FATHERS UNTO THEM, AND THEIR QUEENS SHALL BECOME NURSING MOTHERS; WHEREFORE, THE PROMISES OF THE LORD ARE GREAT UNTO THE GENTILES.

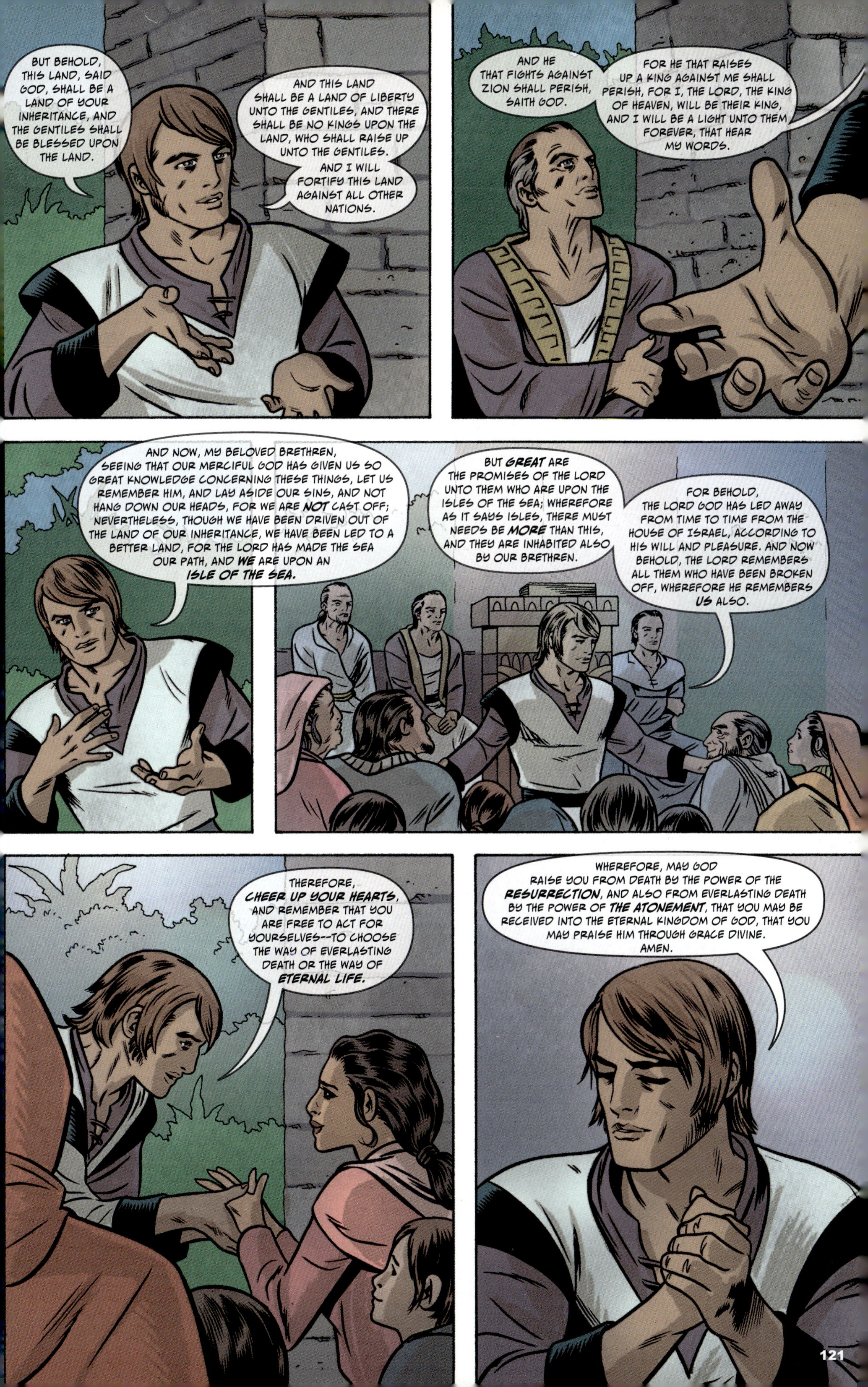
BUT BEHOLD, THIS LAND, SAID GOD, SHALL BE A LAND OF YOUR INHERITANCE, AND THE GENTILES SHALL BE BLESSED UPON THE LAND.
AND THIS LAND SHALL BE A LAND OF LIBERTY UNTO THE GENTILES, AND THERE SHALL BE NO KINGS UPON THE LAND, WHO SHALL RAISE UP UNTO THE GENTILES.
AND I WILL FORTIFY THIS LAND AGAINST ALL OTHER NATIONS.
AND HE THAT FIGHTS AGAINST ZION SHALL PERISH, SAITH GOD.
FOR HE THAT RAISES UP A KING AGAINST ME SHALL PERISH, FOR I, THE LORD, THE KING OF HEAVEN, WILL BE THEIR KING, AND I WILL BE A LIGHT UNTO THEM FOREVER, THAT HEAR MY WORDS.
AND NOW, MY BELOVED BRETHREN, SEEING THAT OUR MERCIFUL GOD HAS GIVEN US SO GREAT KNOWLEDGE CONCERNING THESE THINGS, LET US REMEMBER HIM, AND LAY ASIDE OUR SINS, AND NOT HANG DOWN OUR HEADS, FOR WE ARE ***NOT*** CAST OFF; NEVERTHELESS, THOUGH WE HAVE BEEN DRIVEN OUT OF THE LAND OF OUR INHERITANCE, WE HAVE BEEN LED TO A BETTER LAND, FOR THE LORD HAS MADE THE SEA OUR PATH, AND ***WE*** ARE UPON AN ***ISLE OF THE SEA.***
BUT ***GREAT*** ARE THE PROMISES OF THE LORD UNTO THEM WHO ARE UPON THE ISLES OF THE SEA; WHEREFORE AS IT SAYS ISLES, THERE MUST NEEDS BE ***MORE*** THAN THIS, AND THEY ARE INHABITED ALSO BY OUR BRETHREN.
FOR BEHOLD, THE LORD GOD HAS LED AWAY FROM TIME TO TIME FROM THE HOUSE OF ISRAEL, ACCORDING TO HIS WILL AND PLEASURE. AND NOW BEHOLD, THE LORD REMEMBERS ALL THEM WHO HAVE BEEN BROKEN OFF, WHEREFORE HE REMEMBERS ***US*** ALSO.
THEREFORE, ***CHEER UP YOUR HEARTS***, AND REMEMBER THAT YOU ARE FREE TO ACT FOR YOURSELVES--TO CHOOSE THE WAY OF EVERLASTING DEATH OR THE WAY OF ***ETERNAL LIFE.***
WHEREFORE, MAY GOD RAISE YOU FROM DEATH BY THE POWER OF THE ***RESURRECTION***, AND ALSO FROM EVERLASTING DEATH BY THE POWER OF ***THE ATONEMENT***, THAT YOU MAY BE RECEIVED INTO THE ETERNAL KINGDOM OF GOD, THAT YOU MAY PRAISE HIM THROUGH GRACE DIVINE. AMEN.

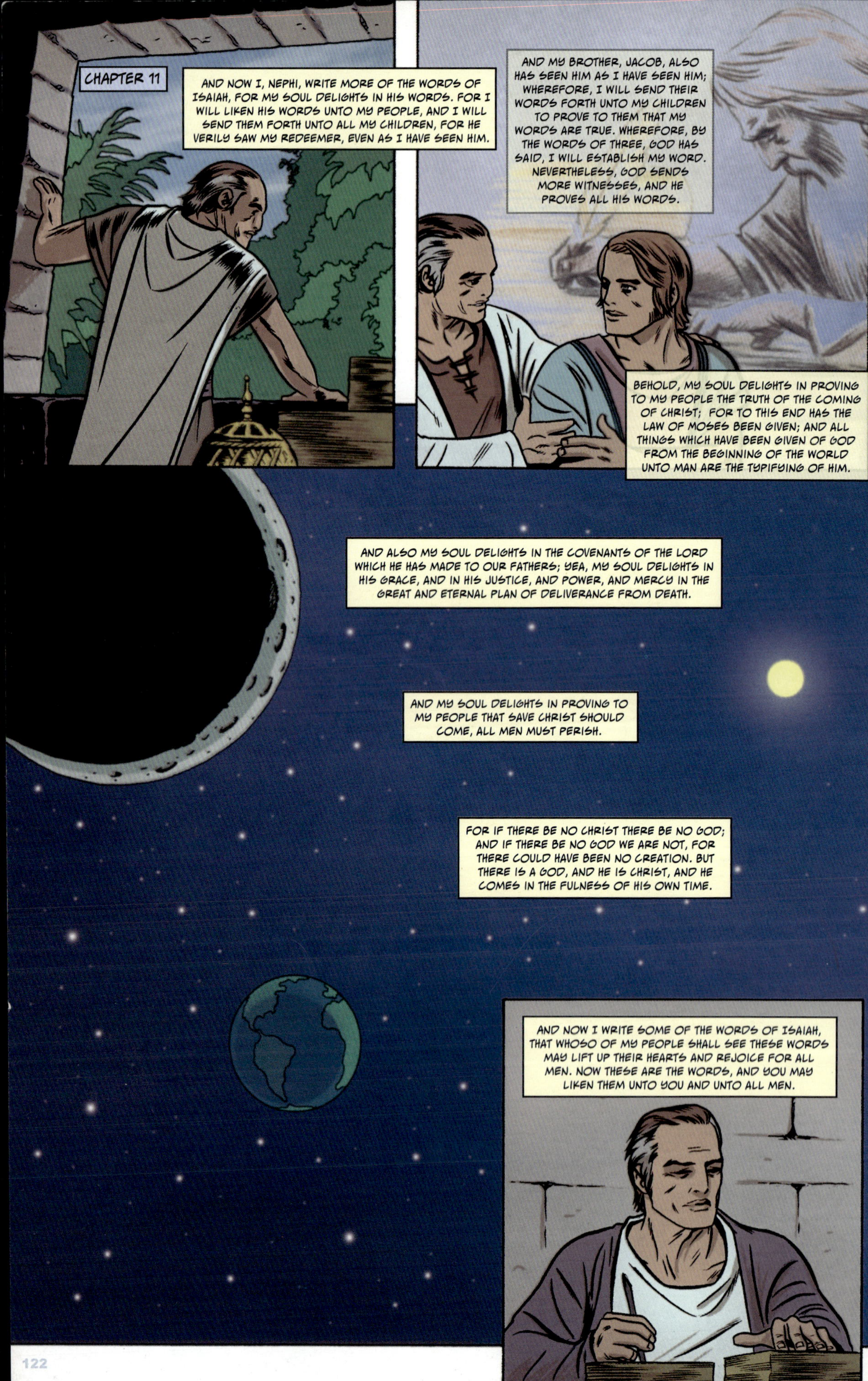
CHAPTER 11
AND NOW I, NEPHI, WRITE MORE OF THE WORDS OF ISAIAH, FOR MY SOUL DELIGHTS IN HIS WORDS. FOR I WILL LIKEN HIS WORDS UNTO MY PEOPLE, AND I WILL SEND THEM FORTH UNTO ALL MY CHILDREN, FOR HE VERILY SAW MY REDEEMER, EVEN AS I HAVE SEEN HIM.
AND MY BROTHER, JACOB, ALSO HAS SEEN HIM AS I HAVE SEEN HIM; WHEREFORE, I WILL SEND THEIR WORDS FORTH UNTO MY CHILDREN TO PROVE TO THEM THAT MY WORDS ARE TRUE. WHEREFORE, BY THE WORDS OF THREE, GOD HAS SAID, I WILL ESTABLISH MY WORD. NEVERTHELESS, GOD SENDS MORE WITNESSES, AND HE PROVES ALL HIS WORDS.
BEHOLD, MY SOUL DELIGHTS IN PROVING TO MY PEOPLE THE TRUTH OF THE COMING OF CHRIST; FOR TO THIS END HAS THE LAW OF MOSES BEEN GIVEN; AND ALL THINGS WHICH HAVE BEEN GIVEN OF GOD FROM THE BEGINNING OF THE WORLD UNTO MAN ARE THE TYPIFYING OF HIM.
AND ALSO MY SOUL DELIGHTS IN THE COVENANTS OF THE LORD WHICH HE HAS MADE TO OUR FATHERS; YEA, MY SOUL DELIGHTS IN HIS GRACE, AND IN HIS JUSTICE, AND POWER, AND MERCY IN THE GREAT AND ETERNAL PLAN OF DELIVERANCE FROM DEATH.
AND MY SOUL DELIGHTS IN PROVING TO MY PEOPLE THAT SAVE CHRIST SHOULD COME, ALL MEN MUST PERISH.
FOR IF THERE BE NO CHRIST THERE BE NO GOD; AND IF THERE BE NO GOD WE ARE NOT, FOR THERE COULD HAVE BEEN NO CREATION. BUT THERE IS A GOD, AND HE IS CHRIST, AND HE COMES IN THE FULNESS OF HIS OWN TIME.
AND NOW I WRITE SOME OF THE WORDS OF ISAIAH, THAT WHOSO OF MY PEOPLE SHALL SEE THESE WORDS MAY LIFT UP THEIR HEARTS AND REJOICE FOR ALL MEN. NOW THESE ARE THE WORDS, AND YOU MAY LIKEN THEM UNTO YOU AND UNTO ALL MEN.

CHAPTER 12
AND IT SHALL COME TO PASS IN THE LAST DAYS, THAT THE MOUNTAIN OF THE LORD'S HOUSE SHALL BE ESTABLISHED IN THE TOP OF THE MOUNTAINS AND SHALL BE EXALTED ABOVE THE HILLS, AND ALL NATIONS SHALL FLOW UNTO IT.
AND MANY PEOPLE SHALL GO AND SAY, COME YE, AND LET US GO UP TO THE MOUNTAIN OF THE LORD, TO THE HOUSE OF THE GOD OF JACOB; AND HE WILL TEACH US OF HIS WAYS, AND WE WILL WALK IN HIS PATHS, FOR OUT OF ZION SHALL GO FORTH THE LAW, AND THE WORD OF THE LORD FROM JERUSALEM.
CHAPTER 13
FOR JERUSALEM IS RUINED, AND JUDAH IS FALLEN, BECAUSE THEIR TONGUES AND THEIR DOINGS HAVE BEEN AGAINST THE LORD, TO PROVOKE THE EYES OF HIS GLORY.
CHAPTER 14
IN THAT DAY SHALL THE BRANCH OF THE LORD BE BEAUTIFUL AND GLORIOUS AND THE FRUIT OF THE EARTH EXCELLENT AND COMELY TO THEM THAT ARE ESCAPED OF ISRAEL.
CHAPTER 15
WO UNTO THEM THAT CALL EVIL GOOD, AND GOOD EVIL, THAT PUT DARKNESS FOR LIGHT, AND LIGHT FOR DARKNESS, THAT PUT BITTER FOR SWEET, AND SWEET FOR BITTER!
AND HE WILL LIFT UP AN ENSIGN TO THE NATIONS FROM FAR, AND WILL HISS UNTO THEM FROM THE END OF THE EARTH; AND BEHOLD, THEY SHALL COME WITH SPEED SWIFTLY; NONE SHALL BE WEARY NOR STUMBLE AMONG THEM.
CHAPTER 16
ALSO I HEARD THE VOICE OF THE LORD, SAYING: WHOM SHALL I SEND, AND WHO WILL GO FOR US? THEN I SAID: HERE AM I; SEND ME.
CHAPTER 17
THEREFORE, THE LORD HIMSELF SHALL GIVE YOU A SIGN--BEHOLD, A VIRGIN SHALL CONCEIVE, AND SHALL BEAR A SON, AND SHALL CALL HIS NAME IMMANUEL.
BUTTER AND HONEY SHALL HE EAT, THAT HE MAY KNOW TO REFUSE THE EVIL AND TO CHOOSE THE GOOD.

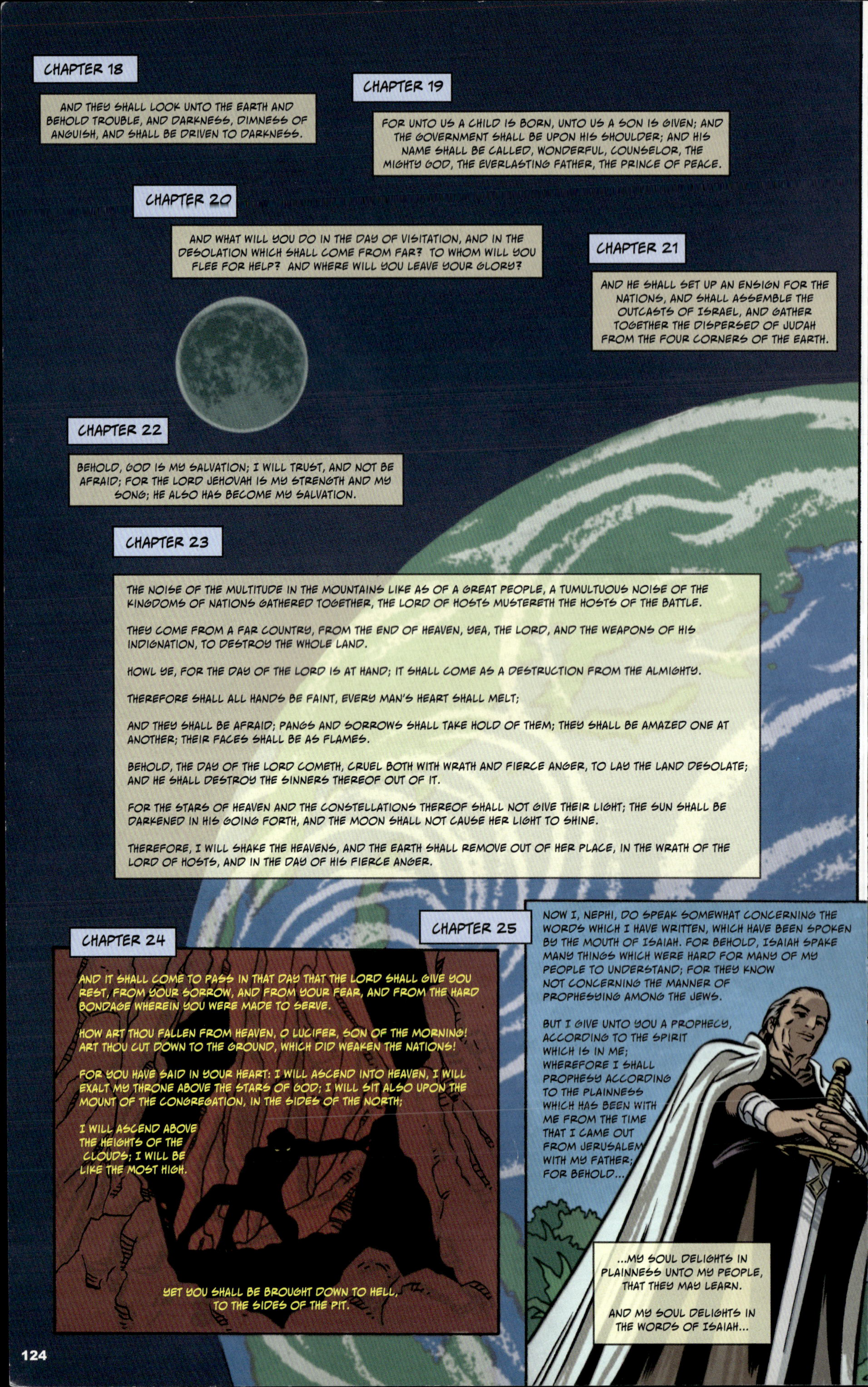
CHAPTER 18
AND THEY SHALL LOOK UNTO THE EARTH AND BEHOLD TROUBLE, AND DARKNESS, DIMNESS OF ANGUISH, AND SHALL BE DRIVEN TO DARKNESS.
CHAPTER 19
FOR UNTO US A CHILD IS BORN, UNTO US A SON IS GIVEN; AND THE GOVERNMENT SHALL BE UPON HIS SHOULDER; AND HIS NAME SHALL BE CALLED, WONDERFUL, COUNSELOR, THE MIGHTY GOD, THE EVERLASTING FATHER, THE PRINCE OF PEACE.
CHAPTER 20
AND WHAT WILL YOU DO IN THE DAY OF VISITATION, AND IN THE DESOLATION WHICH SHALL COME FROM FAR? TO WHOM WILL YOU FLEE FOR HELP? AND WHERE WILL YOU LEAVE YOUR GLORY?
CHAPTER 21
AND HE SHALL SET UP AN ENSIGN FOR THE NATIONS, AND SHALL ASSEMBLE THE OUTCASTS OF ISRAEL, AND GATHER TOGETHER THE DISPERSED OF JUDAH FROM THE FOUR CORNERS OF THE EARTH.
CHAPTER 22
BEHOLD, GOD IS MY SALVATION; I WILL TRUST, AND NOT BE AFRAID; FOR THE LORD JEHOVAH IS MY STRENGTH AND MY SONG; HE ALSO HAS BECOME MY SALVATION.
CHAPTER 23
THE NOISE OF THE MULTITUDE IN THE MOUNTAINS LIKE AS OF A GREAT PEOPLE, A TUMULTUOUS NOISE OF THE KINGDOMS OF NATIONS GATHERED TOGETHER, THE LORD OF HOSTS MUSTERETH THE HOSTS OF THE BATTLE.
THEY COME FROM A FAR COUNTRY, FROM THE END OF HEAVEN, YEA, THE LORD, AND THE WEAPONS OF HIS INDIGNATION, TO DESTROY THE WHOLE LAND.
HOWL YE, FOR THE DAY OF THE LORD IS AT HAND; IT SHALL COME AS A DESTRUCTION FROM THE ALMIGHTY.
THEREFORE SHALL ALL HANDS BE FAINT, EVERY MAN'S HEART SHALL MELT;
AND THEY SHALL BE AFRAID; PANGS AND SORROWS SHALL TAKE HOLD OF THEM; THEY SHALL BE AMAZED ONE AT ANOTHER; THEIR FACES SHALL BE AS FLAMES.
BEHOLD, THE DAY OF THE LORD COMETH, CRUEL BOTH WITH WRATH AND FIERCE ANGER, TO LAY THE LAND DESOLATE; AND HE SHALL DESTROY THE SINNERS THEREOF OUT OF IT.
FOR THE STARS OF HEAVEN AND THE CONSTELLATIONS THEREOF SHALL NOT GIVE THEIR LIGHT; THE SUN SHALL BE DARKENED IN HIS GOING FORTH, AND THE MOON SHALL NOT CAUSE HER LIGHT TO SHINE.
THEREFORE, I WILL SHAKE THE HEAVENS, AND THE EARTH SHALL REMOVE OUT OF HER PLACE, IN THE WRATH OF THE LORD OF HOSTS, AND IN THE DAY OF HIS FIERCE ANGER.
CHAPTER 24
AND IT SHALL COME TO PASS IN THAT DAY THAT THE LORD SHALL GIVE YOU REST, FROM YOUR SORROW, AND FROM YOUR FEAR, AND FROM THE HARD BONDAGE WHEREIN YOU WERE MADE TO SERVE.
HOW ART THOU FALLEN FROM HEAVEN, O LUCIFER, SON OF THE MORNING! ART THOU CUT DOWN TO THE GROUND, WHICH DID WEAKEN THE NATIONS!
FOR YOU HAVE SAID IN YOUR HEART: I WILL ASCEND INTO HEAVEN, I WILL EXALT MY THRONE ABOVE THE STARS OF GOD; I WILL SIT ALSO UPON THE MOUNT OF THE CONGREGATION, IN THE SIDES OF THE NORTH;
I WILL ASCEND ABOVE THE HEIGHTS OF THE CLOUDS; I WILL BE LIKE THE MOST HIGH.
YET YOU SHALL BE BROUGHT DOWN TO HELL, TO THE SIDES OF THE PIT.
CHAPTER 25
NOW I, NEPHI, DO SPEAK SOMEWHAT CONCERNING THE WORDS WHICH I HAVE WRITTEN, WHICH HAVE BEEN SPOKEN BY THE MOUTH OF ISAIAH. FOR BEHOLD, ISAIAH SPAKE MANY THINGS WHICH WERE HARD FOR MANY OF MY PEOPLE TO UNDERSTAND; FOR THEY KNOW NOT CONCERNING THE MANNER OF PROPHESYING AMONG THE JEWS.
BUT I GIVE UNTO YOU A PROPHECY, ACCORDING TO THE SPIRIT WHICH IS IN ME; WHEREFORE I SHALL PROPHESY ACCORDING TO THE PLAINNESS WHICH HAS BEEN WITH ME FROM THE TIME THAT I CAME OUT FROM JERUSALEM WITH MY FATHER; FOR BEHOLD...
...MY SOUL DELIGHTS IN PLAINNESS UNTO MY PEOPLE, THAT THEY MAY LEARN.
AND MY SOUL DELIGHTS IN THE WORDS OF ISAIAH...

...BUT BEHOLD, I PROCEED WITH MY OWN PROPHECY, ACCORDING TO MY PLAINNESS; IN THE WHICH I KNOW THAT NO MAN CAN ERR; NEVERTHELESS, IN THE DAYS THAT THE PROPHECIES OF ISAIAH SHALL BE FULFILLED MEN SHALL KNOW OF A SURETY, AT THE TIMES WHEN THEY SHALL COME TO PASS.
WHEREFORE, THEY ARE OF WORTH UNTO THE CHILDREN OF MEN, AND HE THAT SUPPOSES THAT THEY ARE NOT, UNTO THEM WILL I SPEAK PARTICULARLY, AND CONFINE THE WORDS UNTO MINE OWN PEOPLE; FOR I KNOW THAT THEY SHALL BE OF GREAT WORTH UNTO THEM IN THE LAST DAYS; FOR IN THAT DAY SHALL THEY UNDERSTAND THEM; WHEREFORE, FOR THEIR GOOD HAVE I WRITTEN THEM.
AND NOW THIS I SPEAK BECAUSE OF THE SPIRIT WHICH IS IN ME. AND NOTWITHSTANDING THEY HAVE BEEN CARRIED AWAY THEY SHALL RETURN AGAIN, AND POSSESS THE LAND OF JERUSALEM; WHEREFORE, THEY SHALL BE RESTORED AGAIN TO THE LAND OF THEIR INHERITANCE.
BUT, BEHOLD, THEY SHALL HAVE WARS, AND RUMORS OF WARS; AND WHEN THE DAY COMES THAT THE ONLY BEGOTTEN OF THE FATHER, YEA, EVEN THE FATHER OF HEAVEN AND OF EARTH, SHALL MANIFEST HIMSELF UNTO THEM IN THE FLESH, BEHOLD, THEY WILL REJECT HIM, BECAUSE OF THEIR INIQUITIES, AND THE HARDNESS OF THEIR HEARTS, AND THE STIFFNESS OF THEIR NECKS.

BEHOLD, THEY WILL CRUCIFY HIM; AND AFTER HE IS LAID IN A SEPULCHRE FOR THE SPACE OF THREE DAYS HE SHALL RISE FROM THE DEAD, WITH HEALING IN HIS WINGS; AND ALL THOSE WHO SHALL BELIEVE ON HIS NAME SHALL BE SAVED IN THE KINGDOM OF GOD. WHEREFORE, MY SOUL DELIGHTS TO PROPHESY CONCERNING HIM, FOR I HAVE SEEN HIS DAY, AND MY HEART DOES MAGNIFY HIS HOLY NAME.
AND BEHOLD IT SHALL COME TO PASS THAT AFTER THE MESSIAH HAS RISEN FROM THE DEAD, AND HAS MANIFESTED HIMSELF UNTO HIS PEOPLE, UNTO AS MANY AS WILL BELIEVE ON HIS NAME, BEHOLD, JERUSALEM SHALL BE DESTROYED AGAIN; FOR WOE UNTO THEM THAT FIGHT AGAINST GOD AND THE PEOPLE OF HIS CHURCH.

AND THE LORD WILL SET HIS HAND AGAIN THE SECOND TIME TO RESTORE HIS PEOPLE FROM THEIR LOST AND FALLEN STATE. WHEREFORE, HE WILL PROCEED TO DO A MARVELOUS WORK AND A WONDER AMONG THE CHILDREN OF MEN.
WHEREFORE, HE SHALL BRING FORTH HIS WORDS UNTO THEM, WHICH WORDS SHALL JUDGE THEM AT THE LAST DAY, FOR THEY SHALL BE GIVEN THEM FOR THE PURPOSE OF CONVINCING THEM OF THE TRUE MESSIAH, WHO WAS REJECTED BY THEM; AND UNTO THE CONVINCING OF THEM THAT THEY NEED NOT LOOK FORWARD ANY MORE FOR A MESSIAH TO COME, FOR THERE SHOULD NOT ANY COME, SAVE IT SHOULD BE A FALSE MESSIAH WHICH SHOULD DECEIVE THE PEOPLE; FOR THERE IS SAVE ONE MESSIAH SPOKEN OF BY THE PROPHETS, AND THAT MESSIAH IS HE WHO SHOULD BE REJECTED OF THE JEWS.
FOR ACCORDING TO THE WORDS OF THE PROPHETS, THE MESSIAH COMETH IN SIX HUNDRED YEARS FROM THE TIME THAT MY FATHER LEFT JERUSALEM; AND ACCORDING TO THE WORDS OF THE PROPHETS, AND ALSO THE WORD OF THE ANGEL OF GOD, HIS NAME SHALL BE ***JESUS CHRIST, THE SON OF GOD***.
AND AS THE LORD GOD LIVETH, THERE IS NONE OTHER NAME GIVEN UNDER HEAVEN SAVE IT BE THIS JESUS CHRIST, OF WHICH I HAVE SPOKEN, WHEREBY MAN CAN BE SAVED.
WHEREFORE, THESE THINGS SHALL GO FROM GENERATION TO GENERATION AS LONG AS THE EARTH SHALL STAND; AND THEY SHALL GO ACCORDING TO THE WILL AND PLEASURE OF GOD; AND THE NATIONS WHO SHALL POSSESS THEM SHALL BE JUDGED OF THEM ACCORDING TO THE WORDS WHICH ARE WRITTEN.
FOR WE LABOR DILIGENTLY TO WRITE, TO PERSUADE OUR CHILDREN, AND ALSO OUR BRETHREN, TO BELIEVE IN CHRIST, AND TO BE RECONCILED TO GOD; FOR WE KNOW THAT ***IT IS BY GRACE THAT WE ARE SAVED, AFTER ALL WE CAN DO.***
AND WE TALK OF CHRIST, WE REJOICE IN CHRIST, WE PREACH OF CHRIST, WE PROPHESY OF CHRIST, AND WE WRITE ACCORDING TO OUR PROPHECIES, THAT OUR CHILDREN MAY KNOW TO WHAT SOURCE THEY MAY LOOK FOR A REMISSION OF THEIR SINS.
CHAPTER 26
AND AFTER CHRIST SHALL HAVE RISEN FROM THE DEAD HE SHALL SHOW HIMSELF UNTO YOU, MY CHILDREN, AND MY BELOVED BRETHREN; AND THE WORDS WHICH HE SHALL SPEAK UNTO YOU SHALL BE THE LAW WHICH YE SHALL DO.
AND AFTER THE MESSIAH SHALL COME THERE SHALL BE SIGNS GIVEN UNTO MY PEOPLE OF HIS BIRTH, AND ALSO OF HIS DEATH AND RESURRECTION; AND GREAT AND TERRIBLE SHALL THAT DAY BE UNTO THE WICKED, FOR THEY SHALL PERISH; AND THEY PERISH BECAUSE THEY CAST OUT THE PROPHETS, AND THE SAINTS, AND STONE THEM, AND SLAY THEM; WHEREFORE THE CRY OF THE BLOOD OF THE SAINTS SHALL ASCEND UP TO GOD FROM THE GROUND AGAINST THEM.
O THE PAIN, AND THE ANGUISH OF MY SOUL FOR THE LOSS OF THE SLAIN OF MY PEOPLE! FOR I, NEPHI, HAVE SEEN IT, AND IT WELL NIGH CONSUMETH ME BEFORE THE PRESENCE OF THE LORD; BUT I MUST CRY UNTO MY GOD: THY WAYS ARE JUST.
BUT BEHOLD, THE RIGHTEOUS THAT HEARKEN UNTO THE WORDS OF THE PROPHETS, AND DESTROY THEM NOT, BUT LOOK FORWARD UNTO CHRIST WITH STEADFASTNESS FOR THE SIGNS WHICH ARE GIVEN, NOTWITHSTANDING ALL PERSECUTION--BEHOLD, THEY ARE THEY WHICH SHALL NOT PERISH.
BUT THE SON OF RIGHTEOUSNESS SHALL APPEAR UNTO THEM; AND HE SHALL HEAL THEM, AND THEY SHALL HAVE PEACE WITH HIM, UNTIL THREE GENERATIONS SHALL HAVE PASSED AWAY, AND MANY OF THE FOURTH GENERATION SHALL HAVE PASSED AWAY IN RIGHTEOUSNESS.
AND WHEN THESE THINGS HAVE PASSED AWAY A SPEEDY DESTRUCTION WILL COME UNTO MY PEOPLE; FOR, NOTWITHSTANDING THE PAINS OF MY SOUL, I HAVE SEEN IT; WHEREFORE, I KNOW THAT IT SHALL COME TO PASS; AND THEY SELL THEMSELVES FOR NAUGHT; FOR THE REWARD OF THEIR PRIDE AND THEIR FOOLISHNESS THEY SHALL REAP DESTRUCTION; FOR BECAUSE THEY YIELD UNTO THE DEVIL AND CHOOSE WORKS OF DARKNESS RATHER THAN LIGHT, THEREFORE THEY MUST GO DOWN TO HELL.
FOR THE SPIRIT OF THE LORD WILL NOT ALWAYS STRIVE WITH MAN. AND WHEN THE SPIRIT CEASES TO STRIVE WITH MAN THEN COMES SPEEDY DESTRUCTION, AND THIS GRIEVES MY SOUL.
AND AS I SPAKE CONCERNING THE CONVINCING OF THE JEWS, THAT JESUS IS THE VERY CHRIST, IT MUST NEEDS BE THAT THE GENTILES BE CONVINCED ALSO THAT JESUS IS THE CHRIST, THE ETERNAL GOD;
AND THAT HE MANIFESTS HIMSELF UNTO ALL THOSE WHO BELIEVE IN HIM, BY THE POWER OF THE HOLY GHOST; YEA, UNTO EVERY NATION, KINDRED, TONGUE, AND PEOPLE, WORKING MIGHTY MIRACLES, SIGNS, AND WONDERS, AMONG THE CHILDREN OF MEN ACCORDING TO THEIR FAITH.
FOR THUS SAITH THE LORD GOD: THEY SHALL WRITE THE THINGS WHICH SHALL BE DONE AMONG THEM, AND THEY SHALL BE WRITTEN AND SEALED UP IN A BOOK, AND THOSE WHO HAVE DWINDLED IN UNBELIEF SHALL NOT HAVE THEM, FOR THEY SEEK TO DESTROY THE THINGS OF GOD.

AND THERE ARE ALSO SECRET COMBINATIONS, EVEN AS IN TIMES OF OLD, ACCORDING TO THE COMBINATIONS OF THE DEVIL, FOR HE IS THE FOUNDER OF ALL THESE THINGS, THE FOUNDER OF MURDER, AND WORKS OF DARKNESS AND HE LEADS THEM BY THE NECK WITH A FLAXEN CORD UNTIL HE BINDS THEM WITH HIS STRONG CORDS FOREVER.
HE COMMANDS THAT THERE SHALL BE NO PRIEST-CRAFTS; FOR, BEHOLD, PRIESTCRAFTS ARE THAT MEN PREACH AND SET THEMSELVES UP FOR A LIGHT UNTO THE WORLD, THAT THEY MAY GET GAIN AND PRAISE OF THE WORLD; BUT THEY SEEK NOT THE WELFARE OF ZION.
CHAPTER 27
BUT, BEHOLD, IN THE LAST DAYS, OR IN THE DAYS OF THE GENTILES, ALL THE NATIONS OF THE GENTILES AND ALSO THE JEWS, BOTH THOSE WHO SHALL COME UPON THIS LAND AND THOSE WHO SHALL BE UPON OTHER LANDS, EVEN UPON ALL THE LANDS OF THE EARTH, THEY WILL BE DRUNKEN WITH INIQUITY AND ALL MANNER OF ABOMINATIONS.
AND IT SHALL COME TO PASS THAT THE LORD GOD SHALL BRING FORTH UNTO YOU THE WORDS OF A BOOK, AND THEY SHALL BE THE WORDS OF THEM WHICH HAVE SLUMBERED.
AND BEHOLD THE BOOK SHALL BE SEALED; AND IN THE BOOK SHALL BE A REVELATION FROM GOD, FROM THE BEGINNING OF THE WORLD TO THE ENDING THEREOF.
WHEREFORE, BECAUSE OF THE THINGS WHICH ARE SEALED UP, THE THINGS WHICH ARE SEALED SHALL NOT BE DELIVERED IN THE DAY OF THE WICKEDNESS AND ABOMINATIONS OF THE PEOPLE. WHEREFORE THE BOOK SHALL BE KEPT FROM THEM.
BUT THE BOOK SHALL BE DELIVERED UNTO A MAN, AND HE SHALL DELIVER THE WORDS OF THE BOOK, WHICH ARE THE WORDS OF THOSE WHO HAVE SLUMBERED IN THE DUST, AND HE SHALL DELIVER THESE WORDS UNTO ANOTHER...
...BUT THE WORDS WHICH ARE SEALED HE SHALL NOT DELIVER, NEITHER SHALL HE DELIVER THE BOOK. FOR THE BOOK SHALL BE SEALED BY THE POWER OF GOD, AND THE REVELATION WHICH WAS SEALED SHALL BE KEPT IN THE BOOK UNTIL THE OWN DUE TIME OF THE LORD, THAT THEY MAY COME FORTH; FOR BEHOLD, THEY REVEAL ALL THINGS FROM THE FOUNDATION OF THE WORLD UNTO THE END THEREOF.
AND THE DAY COMES THAT THE WORDS OF THE BOOK WHICH WERE SEALED SHALL BE READ UPON THE HOUSE TOPS; AND THEY SHALL BE READ BY THE POWER OF CHRIST; AND ALL THINGS SHALL BE REVEALED UNTO THE CHILDREN OF MEN WHICH EVER HAVE BEEN AMONG THE CHILDREN OF MEN, AND WHICH EVER WILL BE EVEN UNTO THE END OF THE EARTH.

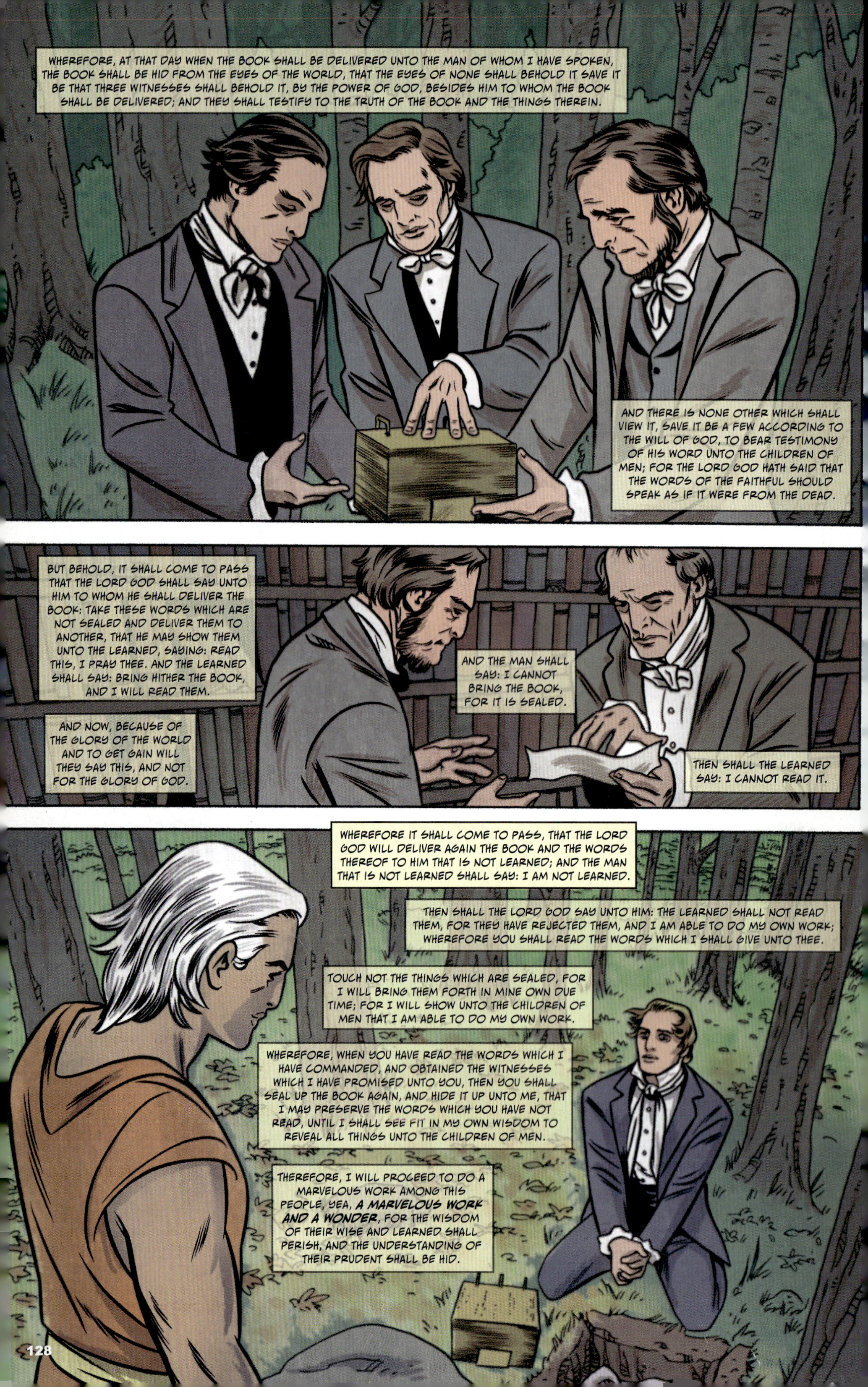
WHEREFORE, AT THAT DAY WHEN THE BOOK SHALL BE DELIVERED UNTO THE MAN OF WHOM I HAVE SPOKEN, THE BOOK SHALL BE HID FROM THE EYES OF THE WORLD, THAT THE EYES OF NONE SHALL BEHOLD IT SAVE IT BE THAT THREE WITNESSES SHALL BEHOLD IT, BY THE POWER OF GOD, BESIDES HIM TO WHOM THE BOOK SHALL BE DELIVERED; AND THEY SHALL TESTIFY TO THE TRUTH OF THE BOOK AND THE THINGS THEREIN.
AND THERE IS NONE OTHER WHICH SHALL VIEW IT, SAVE IT BE A FEW ACCORDING TO THE WILL OF GOD, TO BEAR TESTIMONY OF HIS WORD UNTO THE CHILDREN OF MEN; FOR THE LORD GOD HATH SAID THAT THE WORDS OF THE FAITHFUL SHOULD SPEAK AS IF IT WERE FROM THE DEAD.
BUT BEHOLD, IT SHALL COME TO PASS THAT THE LORD GOD SHALL SAY UNTO HIM TO WHOM HE SHALL DELIVER THE BOOK: TAKE THESE WORDS WHICH ARE NOT SEALED AND DELIVER THEM TO ANOTHER, THAT HE MAY SHOW THEM UNTO THE LEARNED, SAYING: READ THIS, I PRAY THEE. AND THE LEARNED SHALL SAY: BRING HITHER THE BOOK, AND I WILL READ THEM.
AND NOW, BECAUSE OF THE GLORY OF THE WORLD AND TO GET GAIN WILL THEY SAY THIS, AND NOT FOR THE GLORY OF GOD.
AND THE MAN SHALL SAY: I CANNOT BRING THE BOOK, FOR IT IS SEALED.
THEN SHALL THE LEARNED SAY: I CANNOT READ IT.
WHEREFORE IT SHALL COME TO PASS, THAT THE LORD GOD WILL DELIVER AGAIN THE BOOK AND THE WORDS THEREOF TO HIM THAT IS NOT LEARNED; AND THE MAN THAT IS NOT LEARNED SHALL SAY: I AM NOT LEARNED.
THEN SHALL THE LORD GOD SAY UNTO HIM: THE LEARNED SHALL NOT READ THEM, FOR THEY HAVE REJECTED THEM, AND I AM ABLE TO DO MY OWN WORK; WHEREFORE YOU SHALL READ THE WORDS WHICH I SHALL GIVE UNTO THEE.
TOUCH NOT THE THINGS WHICH ARE SEALED, FOR I WILL BRING THEM FORTH IN MINE OWN DUE TIME; FOR I WILL SHOW UNTO THE CHILDREN OF MEN THAT I AM ABLE TO DO MY OWN WORK.
WHEREFORE, WHEN YOU HAVE READ THE WORDS WHICH I HAVE COMMANDED, AND OBTAINED THE WITNESSES WHICH I HAVE PROMISED UNTO YOU, THEN YOU SHALL SEAL UP THE BOOK AGAIN, AND HIDE IT UP UNTO ME, THAT I MAY PRESERVE THE WORDS WHICH YOU HAVE NOT READ, UNTIL I SHALL SEE FIT IN MY OWN WISDOM TO REVEAL ALL THINGS UNTO THE CHILDREN OF MEN.
THEREFORE, I WILL PROCEED TO DO A MARVELOUS WORK AMONG THIS PEOPLE, YEA, ***A MARVELOUS WORK AND A WONDER***, FOR THE WISDOM OF THEIR WISE AND LEARNED SHALL PERISH, AND THE UNDERSTANDING OF THEIR PRUDENT SHALL BE HID.